Charles Palliser was born in America but spent most of his adult life in Britain. He took a degree at Oxford and has taught English Studies at the University of Strathclyde in Glasgow since 1974. His first novel, *The Quincunx*, was published by Canongate in 1989. He is currently at work on a new novel.

CHARLES PALLISER

THE SENSATIONIST

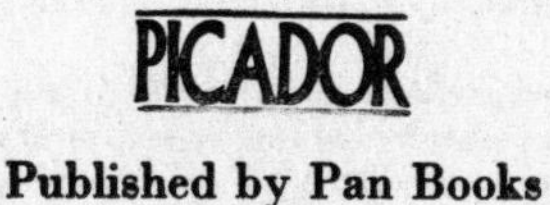

Published by Pan Books

First published 1991 by Jonathan Cape Ltd
This edition first published 1991 by Pan Books Ltd,
Cavaye Place, London SW10 9PG
1 3 5 7 9 8 6 4 2

ISBN 0 330 31843 8
Printed in England by Clays Ltd, St Ives plc

For my closest reader

CHAPTER ONE

HE LOOKED DOWN from the dark room at the street-lamp. Specks of dust danced in its orange glow like tiny flickering moths, appearing and disappearing as they turned over. Above it the sky was black. He didn't hear her come in until she was beside him.

Got everything you need? she said.

He nodded.

She looked out of the window as if curious to see what had attracted his attention. From what she saw, she could not have known what it all meant to him – the very ordinariness of each darkened house, the humped shapes of cars and the pools of light. Have known how it disturbed him with its sense of mystery withheld, of strangeness made familiar, after what, in view of all he had heard of the city, he had expected.

It's a quiet street, isn't it?

She didn't answer. Their elbows touched. She was wearing a dress that left her arms and shoulders bare.

He inhaled. Flowers. Greenness. She'd taken a lot of trouble over the meal.

How far out are we?

Quite a long way, she said. You'll see tomorrow.

Above the roof of the house opposite, the orange glow extended towards the horizon where a faintly purple band of cloud emerged from the darkness. Beyond that a dark outline, perhaps of hills.

As if she'd seen where his gaze was directed, she said:

When it's a clear day you can see the mountains.

She was small and dark. In profile her face was intense, the skin very pale, the eye-lashes long. She was seeing the mountains, perhaps.

I saw them as the plane circled, he told her. He went on to tell her that he was looking forward to getting up there. That it was one of the reasons he had come.

Go before the snow, she said. In fact, why don't we all go.

It was only the end of summer. Of what they called summer. When she turned her head the light from the lamp picked out the highlights in a vivid glow, leaving the hollows black. Somewhere in the flat behind them a tap was turned on, starting a spreading hiss in the pipes that seemed to encircle them. He didn't know how to respond to her words.

Her husband spoke from the door.

What are you doing in the dark?

And he flicked the light on.

He lay in the darkness, his senses sharpened by tiredness,

hearing their voices and watching the transformations of the shadows made by the light coming through the thin curtain as the moon moved in and out of clouds. There was no sound except an occasional car on the main road at the end of the street.

He wondered if he had been asleep. The sounds from the next room had stopped. He drifted into sleep. He dreamed of a school-friend of his whom he hadn't seen for many years, had scarcely thought of, whom he now saw drowning in front of him, crying out speechlessly, his white legs descending an invisible stair-way.

Magnus drove him in. It was raining and he gripped the wheel angrily with one hand, holding his cigarette with the other as the car hiccupped between red lights, moving forward in a series of pounces.

Be better once we reach the motorway, he said.

He nodded.

The city disclosed itself as they neared the river. He had seen only the suburbs while he was driven in from the airport last night. Now they were passing along a wide road of tall buildings with a bottom row of shops, most of them shabby or boarded up. Some of the buildings were derelict, their windows gaping blankly. Many of them had been demolished, exposing brickwork that had been hidden for a century or more. The road was long and almost straight. Above the roofs he saw the tops of high blocks and, when they passed a cleared site, he glimpsed their bases rising from grass-covered wastes. This, and the appearance of the pedestrians – bedraggled, beaten, sullen – was what he had expected.

Suddenly they were up on high and moving quickly. Magnus swung the car into the middle lane and accelerated, then leaned forward and vigorously wiped the windscreen. The city was spread out before and around him. They were above all but the tallest buildings now. To the left were the cranes of the docks marking the line of the river. The view to the right was blocked by a small lorry keeping noisily abreast.

We're over there, said Magnus, indicating with his jaw a direction ahead and slightly to the left.

He had only a moment to try to make sense of the endless roofs far away through the rain. He saw patches of green and a large black building on top of a hill. Through the piers of the bridge he caught glimpses of water. The surface of the road gleamed blackly. Then they were swooping down into a tunnel, white-tiled, lamps glowing, like a monstrous urinal. Then out into the watery daylight again as the carriageway passed through a giant forest of stone trees that carried the motorway overhead and emerged at street level.

Here a whole district had been smashed down to make a motorway intersection. Beside them but much lower as they halted at a light, the traffic reverberated at the bottom of a deep canyon.

Magnus turned the car into a quiet road that curved

around the edge of a hill. Tree-lined streets led off it to squares with gardens in the middle. They were in different departments, so when Magnus had parked the car and pointed towards Telling's office, he left him – turning away suddenly and walking stiffly towards a side-entrance.

He had coffee with Telling and then was shown to his office. He remembered him and some of the others from the interview. The work would be interesting, he hoped. That was why he had accepted the job. The place, despite what he had told Lena, had not been an attraction.

He pushed the chair back, holding on to the edge of the desk. He could just see grass and part of a tree beyond the edge of the building opposite. The windows were double-glazed and no sound from outside reached him. From within, beyond his door, he heard the steady click of keyboards. He looked at his watch. His belly was beginning to hurt.

The cafeteria was low and dark, crowded already. He attached himself to the queue that shuffled forward, trays held out, faces fixed ahead. When he had paid he stood, holding his lunch in front of him, searching for a space. He saw Magnus. There was a girl at his table. He carried his tray over. They were talking about a party. Magnus only nodded as he sat down and went on eating as he listened to the girl.

She stopped speaking and smiled at him. He told her his name. She asked him:

Are you looking for somewhere to stay? She was called Anna.

He wanted a flat with no hassle, he told her. And quickly. He hadn't got the time to spend looking.

Why not near here? You don't have to live miles out. She looked at Magnus. This is the Bohemian quarter.

She smiled. She had a beautiful neck.

Go to an agent, Magnus said. This afternoon.

A big man sat down and said something he didn't understand. He asked him to repeat it. He still didn't understand.

The girl explained. An agent would be no use. You needed to hear of somewhere. He had a friend who might have what he wanted. Gretta, she was called. She'd probably be there on Saturday.

Her hair was blonde. She wore a black velvet headband. She was pretty. It was when she smiled that he thought she seemed sad.

Others sat at the table. Some he already knew. He made no attempt to join in the conversation, not always catching what someone said. Magnus he could understand, and Anna.

The big man, whose name was Paul, was giving the party. The others seemed to be teasing him, apparently about a girl. He ate fastidiously. His features, crowded together at the centre of a pale moon of flesh, were small and delicate.

Another man joined them. When they had shaken hands, he said:

Glad to have you on board. He seemed to be imitating someone. He glanced at Magnus and said: We're in the business of foreseeing the unforeseeable. Did Telling say that to you? He smiled.

Telling hadn't said quite that, but he had said something rather similar. You must carry your own weight, he had said. There's no room for passengers.

He started to tell Willi what Telling *had* said, but he wasn't interested.

When he looked at Anna she smiled back as if to show him she had noticed how ill at ease he was. Before he left the table he took Gretta's number in case he didn't make the party on Saturday.

They ate in the kitchen tonight. He had bought a bottle of wine on the way home. He had chosen a good one. It embarrassed them with the meat-balls and fried potatoes. Magnus was sitting slightly sideways against the wall, one leg thrust out, as if anxious to be away. They would have been quarrelling if he hadn't been there, it seemed to him. The fluorescent lighting made them all look hung-over.

How'd it go? Lena asked.

I rang a couple of agents. They weren't hopeful.

Louis and Jan might want someone to take on their place, she said.

I thought of that. I rang them earlier. No answer.

Where is it? I don't want to be a long way out.

Just ten minutes from work, Magnus said, standing up. Then he said: In the Bohemian quarter. I'll try them again.

When Magnus had gone out he said softly:

He doesn't want me here, does he?

Ach no, it's not that. It's nothing to do with you.

She laid her hand on top of his for a moment.

Magnus came in to say there was no answer again.

Nor could he see her in the room where a mass of people, frozen in the dizzying flash of the strobes, jerked from one posture to another. So either she wasn't coming after all or she would be late. It was already after midnight when they'd arrived. He hoped she hadn't been and left. They shouldn't have gone to the restaurant, but he needed to do something for Magnus and Lena.

Their table was in a dark corner. Lena leant her chin on her arms and smiled at him across the candle. She turned her head to Magnus and the light gleamed on the back of her hair. Magnus said very little. He seemed to be angry about something. Lena talked about her time at college, the disappointment of her ambitions, her hopes of getting back to her music. They left the car there and walked. Magnus had drunk a lot. They said they wouldn't stay late.

He saw the big fleshy head of Paul jutting above the others. Sweat streamed down his cheeks as he twisted his body, placing his feet delicately as if treading out a pattern of invisible marks.

He forced his way through to him and shouted:

Isn't Anna coming?

He carried on stamping and twisting his hips, just shrugging slightly. The girl he was with was small, dressed in a tight black skirt that finished high above her knee. Her hair was black. She danced with her eyes half-closed.

He went back to the kitchen and poured himself another whisky. A man was lying on the floor. It looked like Paul's flat-mate. He lit a cigarette. He didn't want to talk to any of the people there. He looked out of the window. A night that was still mild and might have had something to communicate to him down in the streets where the trees were gently swaying to shed their leaves, was being ruined by this blotch of noisy, frightened humanity. He punished himself for being there by rasping hard on the cigarette so that the smoke hurt him. He needed something. He wondered who he could ask.

The flat was spacious with big rooms and high ceilings, but the walls needed painting and the carpets were threadbare. At the door he brushed against a girl coming in.

Enjoying yourself? She smiled.

I could be, he said.

Haven't I met you with Gregory and that crowd?

I don't know a Gregory, he said.

Neither do I. She giggled. She was slim. A bit drunk.

Are you a friend of Paul? she said.

No. I know him through Magnus. I work with him. I've just started.

I don't know Magnus.

Dance? he said and laid his hand lightly on her waist. She nodded and turned towards the other room. He followed, keeping his hand on her. He could feel the warmth of her body. He steered her into the centre of the room and drew her against him.

The music was languorous. An epicene voice sang of a city on the other side of the world, of the sun declining over the gleaming sea and darkness falling, of the short night on a warm beach and the dawn coming up over the mountains.

And here in this cold city in the north he held a stranger's body and they shuffled their feet to the rhythm of the music. Her head nuzzled against him. Her hair blonde and curly and sweet-smelling when he pressed his face into it. Her skirt was very short. He put his hand on her thigh above the skirt. She was in her early twenties. He moved his hand softly on her naked thigh.

Where do you live? he whispered.

Miles away, she said sadly.

Later he said:

Let me ring for a taxi.

She nodded slightly.

In the dim light of the lamp he could see her mouth half open, her teeth between her parted lips.

He moved forward gently.

Nice, nice, he said.

Her hair, spread out behind her, was soft under his elbows. Her breathing quickened.

He pushed hard this time and she gasped. They were balanced on the edge.

Is this nice for you? he asked.

He thought she hadn't heard him, but then she said slowly:

Yes, it is.

But there's even nicer, he said, drawing back.

Shyly she placed a hand on the side of his chest.

The soft rain was almost reassuring against his cheek. In the long street there were few lights. Nobody else had come to wait beside him. No pedestrians had passed and only a few cars. He had no precise idea of where he was, but knew he had to penetrate the centre and get south of the river.

Far away to the left lights appeared, too high for a lorry. It was long before he heard the labouring whine and then, through the darkness and rain, saw the illuminated number. He stepped into the street and it hissed to a halt in front of him.

The light and warmth inside made him suddenly aware of his tiredness. He was the only passenger, unless there was anyone on top. The bus ran along the same street for several miles, then it stopped and then it stopped again, and then again and more frequently as people got on. Postmen, office-cleaners, shift-workers, he supposed. No one spoke, as if by an agreement to preserve what was left of the privacy of sleep from which they had just been expelled. Outside, the light was growing in the bleak streets. The centre was further than he had imagined. The city larger. The suburbs uglier.

CHAPTER TWO

IT HAD STORM-DOORS and the key that operated them was very big. She had difficulty making it work. The inner door had an elaborate design in coloured glass: an ill-drawn Saint George wrapped in the scaly coils of a serpent, his sword appearing to thrust disconcertingly at his own body.

The flat was big and seemed empty though it had quite a lot of furniture. It was dark even when she put the lights on. The floors sloped down to the back of the building. It was four floors up, the top flat.

Settlement, she said, seeing where his gaze was directed. Ages ago.

He looked out of the window. The houses on the opposite side of the street were lower because of the steepness of the hill. Over their roofs he could see the next street – only one line of roofs because after that was the river. Beyond, he could see the trees of the park on the other side. Just opposite was the gate into the park.

It needs painting, she said.

Cold in winter. These big rooms.

The ceiling was a long way above them, dim in the late afternoon gloom, covered in elaborate plaster-work.

Great for parties. You haven't seen the bedrooms yet.

Now there's an idea.

As she came towards the door he put his arm out to bar her way.

Come out with me one night.

She laughed.

Didn't Paul tell you I'm moving in with my friend? That's why I'm giving up this place.

So?

So no chance.

Oh come on. I'm only asking you to a movie. I'm not asking you to fuck.

Yeah, well a fuck would be a lot easier actually. My friend's awful jealous.

As she moved towards the door he lowered his arm as if to let her pass, then caught her by the waist.

Well, Gretta, a fuck can easily be arranged.

He pulled her gently towards him, close enough to kiss, but just held her against him.

So I gather, she said, and put her hands on the back of his neck.

The city was notorious for its poverty and slums, but this district had once been fashionable. It was an area of parks, tree-lined avenues and handsome squares, lying to the west and slightly to the north of the centre along one side of the great shallow valley, sloping down to the river-estuary, on which the city was built. Through the area ran a smaller river in a steep valley between the hills.

The docks, now largely derelict, were far away to the south and it was only occasionally that the sound of fog-horns reached this far up. When he looked out of his bedroom window over the roofs of the next street he could see the tops of the office-blocks in the centre – dimly by day but more clearly when they were illuminated at night.

Though the flat was in a district that was still attractive, two streets eastward the slums began.

You've got to give it everything you've got. *That's what he'd said. There's no room for passengers here. Everyone has to carry their own weight, he'd said.*

I told him I was committed one hundred per cent. He touched my shoulder with his hand and smiled. That was good.

Plus he liked the concept, he said. Telling assured me several times how much he liked the concept.

Much of his time he had to spend in a suite of windowless offices where temperature and humidity were precisely controlled. In the pale neon lighting he fancied he could have been hundreds of feet underground. All the flooring was carpet to absorb sound so that if someone nearby raised their voice, it was lost before it reached him. But at this time nobody raised their voice. The only sounds were the hissing of the ventilation and the humming of the machines.

As they came out of the cinema it was raining. Not hard, but steadily, insidiously. He offered to get a taxi but she shook her head. Her headscarf would keep her dry.

He asked her if she was hungry. She wasn't. But when he asked her to come and have coffee she agreed. His flat was between where they were now and her own flat. On the way they talked about the film. At a busy intersection he took her arm to guide her across. On the other side he let go.

In the flat he turned on the gas-fire in the kitchen. While the kettle was boiling he went into his bedroom and lit the fire.

She took off the scarf and shook the drips out of her hair, laughing. Without her coat, her bare neck and the part of her shoulders that he could see were very beautiful.

She told him she'd been there before to one of Gretta's parties. Paul had taken her. He pointed out the changes he'd made. She was amused by what he'd done in the kitchen, laughing at the way he'd arranged things and at the colour he'd started painting the walls.

She sat at the table and watched him making coffee. They talked about work. Then he asked her about herself. She had been married for a few years, she told him. It ended three years ago. Her accent was soft and seemed quaint to him. She cradled her mug of coffee somewhat timidly, holding it almost under her chin. Since then there'd been nobody in particular. She didn't want to get too involved again for a bit.

She glanced at him nervously. Then she looked at her watch. He let the conversation peter out. At last she stood up. He stood too, and moved close to her before she could reach the door.

Will you stay tonight?

She seemed to reflect for a moment.

Have you got an alarm? she asked.

He nodded. In the bedroom he helped her to take off her clothes. When she was naked he pulled off his own while she lay on the bed. He came into her quickly, whispering her name into her ear. She ran her hand up and down his back, half pulling him into her, half pushing him away.

His tongue fluttered against her lips teasing them open, while his finger and thumb sought access to her nether mouth. *Anna. Anna.*

He woke up aware that he'd slept badly. He saw her head on the other pillow turned away from him. He carefully got out of bed and put on a dressing-gown and slippers without waking her. He went into the kitchen and made himself tea and ate some bread.

After twenty minutes she came into the kitchen dressed. She said:

Why didn't you wake me. I've got to be at work in half-an-hour.

They didn't kiss. He gave her something to eat and drink. She looked older. He resented her presence and wished she hadn't stayed.

He looked out of the window as he stood to wash up. The sky was overcast. In the street people were hurrying past. Schoolboys in bright red uniforms and carrying satchels. Girls in blue.

She insisted on arriving at work before him so he let her go on ahead.

The next day was Saturday. He stood in the front room looking down into the street. The sky was overcast. An old man passing along the pavement gesticulated at some children – black eyes in exquisite dark faces – who were playing with a skipping-rope and blocking the way.

In the afternoon he went to the supermarket across the bridge and bought packets of bacon, tinned fruit, eggs and bread.

Coming back along the great western road in the sunlight which gave no warmth, he thought of the million lives enacted in these few square miles. (Many of them more fulfilling than his own, and among them some, perhaps, with which his might be advantageously involved.) Of the hidden means that made it possible. This eating, heating, excreting. Of the elaborate network of wires and pipes that ran beneath his feet. This slowly evolving organism into which he too was now plugged: roads dug and re-dug like the scarred veins of an addict. And, deeper, the ancient sewers – lightless caverns connected by fetid canals.

And above ground? This street? Arrangements of stone and tar. Metalled usurpers of ancient cart-tracks. Across which on rubber crawled cars, buses, lorries. Amid exhalations of dust. Of grit. And he, feet duly placed, following a course. The path marked out invisibly which he had trodden and would tread.

CHAPTER THREE

BETWEEN THE WHITE bars the squares of blackness yielded nothing. Only when he squeezed himself against the sink to rinse a glass could he see his own reflection and then, as if behind him, the backs of tenements opposite.

Sheltering from the press, he leaned against a poster advertising a Parisian *boîte* of the 1890s. Beside him hung a wicker trellis up which a vine had been encouraged to climb. He looked around him at the little pitifulnesses of good taste which seemed to him to make people's kitchens the most revealing, the most intimate, of all their rooms.

Now filled with strangers, half-strangers. Some faces he recognized from work. Bearded men, couples, fat women shouting. Intimacies of language from which he was excluded. His ear still unadjusted to their speech.

A girl moved past him. He'd noticed her earlier. Her jutting sweater contrasted with her tight-hipped jeans. She poured herself a glass of water. As she drank she seemed to look out as he had done.

Do you think anyone is watching us from across there?

She turned and looked at him curiously. Then with a faint smile she moved away and joined some people by the door.

He poured himself more wine. Metallic. Thin.

The group by the door made way for him. They were doing something, but from here he couldn't see what.

Back in the other room the tang of sweating bodies prickled his nostrils. Gamy. The room vibrated. Shirts hung down over jeans. Hips were swinging. Hands on each other's bodies. The girl he was dancing with avoided his gaze, her thin mouth turned down. An ungenerous face. He moved away when the record changed.

The speakers hammered unrelentingly. He jerked to the rhythm, uncaring of the dancers he bumped. In a minute he'd go back to that distinctive shape – temptingly graspable – he'd noticed among the wine-bottles.

An elbow hit his ribs. He elbowed back. He raised his head to the ceiling where a pattern of changing lights revolved. His shirt stuck to him. He undid the buttons.

He lit a cigarette. Not dancing the music hurt, as if motion absorbed the shock. He hardly knew where he was, who he was. He had to remember to breathe. He knew he hated the party.

But this he needed. This painful darkness, the smell, the heat. The battering rhythm finding an echo in his head, making him strange to himself so that he looked at his hand holding the cigarette as at something wonderful.

The whisky was not the kind he was learning to appreciate. It rasped his throat and left an after-taste of soap. He steadied himself with one arm against the wall.

He looked at a chair. It was blue. Why blue. He felt that if he could know why it was blue he would have the answer to a question that had long preoccupied him but that he couldn't formulate just now. If he knew why blue he could formulate the question. He wanted to share his realization, but the group he approached seemed uninterested. They were uninterested also when he asked them what they were doing.

Staggering, he put out his hand to push against a doorpost. Its surface cool. The shiny paint flaking off in places. Cracks. Solidified streams of superfluous paint.

As he moved away someone bumped him. The girl again. She'd been one of the group in the kitchen.

Her eyes wide open. She was very young. From his own country. A student. Just begun here.

Her unset features pretty, the delicacy of her neck and shoulders where the thin sweater left them bare, the pale lobes of her ears soft like a child's. Her pouting rear from which he restrained his hand but not his gaze.

He wondered if she'd dance. But before he had time to speak a melancholy descended upon him. He could have reached out to take the belt-buckle of her low-hung jeans but he averted his gaze, let her move away for suddenly the room is too hot and crowded.

Feeling the smoothed cobblestones beneath his soles reminds him of the great pebbles of a forgotten beach from his childhood. Beyond the back-greens, the tenements on either side of the lane are dark except for where, at regular spaces, dim bulbs burn on the common stair. Columns of rectangular lights. The air is cool on his face. He lights a cigarette. Makes it rasp as he inhales.

Why the impulse to leave. Alone.

He stops. Still a little drunk, with clarity he sees. The sky clear. The stars sharp against its blackness. Silence.

Around him shelves of sleepers. Each pursuing his or her. And perhaps one of them. But most have chosen. Chosen? *Had* chosen for them. And he? Not too late. Though he feels – if not old, at least not young.

He breathes in. A taste of smoke. A faint anticipation of winter. He kicks a can. Scutters across the cobbles. A cat, hidden in a bush, bolts across the lane in front of him and scrabbles up the wall.

He walked on, pursuing streets that still disclosed the shape of the hill to which the district owed its name.

Between sleep and waking. Dredged towards wakefulness by a sound which had faded, leaving only its scar on his mind, as the whorls of spinning darkness resolved themselves into familiar shapes, he knew that the building was moving like a loose tooth in a rotted gum, that the noise that had woken him was the crack of splitting masonry, and that his bed had lurched towards the opposite wall.

Then panic was succeeded by the awareness that all was normal. The moonlight gleamed behind the curtains. Silence, except for an occasional car on the main road. If the building was sinking, it was doing so very slowly. A century had contributed a few inches. He drifted back into sleep.

It rained every day for weeks as the autumn advanced. Sometimes the stench of a nearby brewery hung over the streets around his flat all day – heavy, sweet, intimate.

He ascended the steep street. It was late afternoon. The trees that lined the terraces of comfortable old tenements quivered together, and the leaves they had shed were slippery on the pavement. A mild wind blew to him a fragrance of summer mingled with a more acrid foretaste of winter. He reached the top of the hill and just before he turned into the next street he realized his solitude.

CHAPTER FOUR

IN HIGH NARROW rooms about the city's western suburbs, their elegance clouded by modern improvements, he discovered an intensity of desire that at first excited him. Amid the glass-topped coffee-tables, the blackly discreet hi-fi systems, and the thick white carpets lapped against the walls like icing, the young wives of his colleagues played hostess. The models taken from what they watched and read were to be outdone for, ambitious to move ever outwards from the tall grey streets of students and immigrants to the spiralling suburbs of gardens and trees where, in squat red terraces, suburban rivalries became clearer, they strained to excel.

At the dinner-parties or supper-parties he was invited to, he envied his colleagues their ease of satisfaction. All in couples, conspiracies against the rest of the world – all satisfaction reduced to one person out of the vast randomness.

The wives flirted with him, but timidly, or with offensive casualness for they were not going to risk what they had gained. He saw their faces slip into middle age –

slackcheeked, heavyjawed, eyes appealing for help: they'd done the right things. Why were they not happy?

His own temptation lay in the fascination of the clear screen, to which point of focus all problems were (he hoped) resolved and within whose frame all could be known and settled. All uncertainties honed to this point, to this steady glow, this unwinking but not judgemental eye.

And other temptations.

Once, as he was coming out of the toilet with a colleague a few paces behind him, Paul came past and said:

Did you make a hit?

Willi smiled.

When he closed his eyes he was as aware of her, though the callous thumping of the music severed them, pasting them, reduced to one dimension, against a screen with all the others dancing. When he looked again her head was held back, her eyes shut, her arms and shoulders dipping as if labouring to the rhythm, her slender hips in the tight skirt swaying less violently. He saw movement beneath the short grey lashes – her eyes, only half-closed, were watching him, the faint smile was for him.

A movement of the tight-packed mass pushed them together and he felt her arms close around his waist, knew she wanted him.

And again later on other occasions, at other parties. One among many he remembered, on the city's edge, where he looked out through a wall of glass – snubbing his own image, gaunt and hollow-eyed – staring instead over his shoulder at the other high blocks and beyond them to the vastness of the sodium-yellow haze ringing the horizon.

Behind him, but mirrored in the glass before him, were people dancing, the girls white-faced, high-cheeked. Turning he saw their uninterest – intuited their frenzied torpor even towards the men the backs of whose necks they dandled their hands against, who themselves laid fingers on the backs of their thighs in the ritualized intimacies of strangers – his own gaze scanning hip-high tight skirts, the vulnerabilities of thighs and knees, of slender calves, all, he knew, mirrored in his own hungry stare. His focus now on eyes evasive, unseeing or not open. A myriad of ramifying potentialities but closed off at each unanswered appeal. Yet now narrowing to one face. That girl gazing at him?

Or a white face with red-smeared lips and hollow eyes emerging from the darkness looking for.

CHAPTER FIVE

IT HAD BEEN a warehouse and the smell of damp, ancient masonry mingled even now with the tartness of oil-paint and turps, reminding that, behind the paper-boarded walls and beneath the squares of industrial carpeting, a decaying building still lurked, dank cellars mocking aspirations doomed to crumble.

A narrow passage led to the main space in the middle of which day entered through a skylight, mercilessly showing up the colours on the canvases. His friends were ahead of him. He caught them up.

Where did you get the catalogue?

Over there.

She pointed towards the entrance where a girl sat at a table. He had walked past without noticing. He went back. She was slender with black hair falling to her shoulders and large eyes. The lashes thick and long. Her eyes were lowered as he approached. They opened, brilliant blue, as his shadow fell over her, and she looked up.

Can I have one?

She smiled, but without looking at him, as she took his money.

He felt his mouth move awkwardly towards a smile. He would have spoken, but others were waiting behind him.

He moved away and looked at the pictures. Studies in the textures and colours of the sea's artefacts. The artist had sought to render the delicacy and precision of unperceiving chance. Translucencies of shell chafed to paper-thinness. Corrugations of rock fretted by the restless tide.

The smile had intrigued him.

Do they work for you? Lindsay said. He hadn't noticed her approach.

He shook his head.

I collected pebbles and shells when I was a child. He shrugged.

Philistine, she said. Let's get a drink.

At the other end of the gallery glasses of wine were being given out. They joined the queue.

He studied with Leven. You can see it, she said.

He kept turning to look at the girl. When she was free she picked up a paperback. At intervals she shook her head so that the long black hair fell in swirls around her neck and shoulders. When they reached the front he handed a glass to Lindsay, and picked up two more. Lindsay said:

He's got one already. Trust him.

He had already noticed that Phillip was standing on the

edge of a group, his glass almost empty. But then she saw where he was looking. She smiled and said:

I see. After a moment she said: I wonder how she got that black eye.

He went over to the entrance. He waited until she was free, then placed it before her.

I hope you prefer red.

She looked up surprised.

I don't want it, she said, half-smiling, as if at a joke he hadn't understood.

He told her, in that case he didn't know what to do with it.

The smile grew wider. Her mouth was too large for beauty, perhaps, but it was the most expressive and generous smile he had seen. There was a faint bruise high up on her right cheek and darkness under the eye.

Then I'll take it and thank you, she said.

After tasting it very quickly with a delicate, beak-like action of the lips, she placed it beside her and bent her head over her book.

What do you think of the paintings?

She looked up as if astonished he was still there.

I haven't had time to look at them.

That's a shame. Do they keep you so busy?

She was still looking up at him. She thrust her jaw forward. Her slight smile was watchful, amused.

Not that busy. I'll see them before I go. Anyway, I know his paintings well.

How long have you worked here? he asked.

For a moment she studied his face with a slight frown, then as if she'd solved a problem and was suddenly bored by it, she said:

Two years, if you want to know. She put her book down and said: There are other people waiting.

He stood aside until she'd sold them what they wanted. Then he said:

I'd like to know your name.

He'd lost her. She said:

Don't you think you're being rather impertinent?

Her tone was pleasant, inquisitive.

He said:

Mine's David.

Don't you think you're being rather impertinent, David?

He shrugged and walked away. Later he looked over towards her several times. Her head was bent over the book. The level of wine in the glass beside her was no lower.

As they were leaving Lindsay said:

Did you notice David making a pass at that girl?

What's her name? he asked.

They didn't know.

I believe she was married, Lindsay said. And I think I've seen her with a child.

Since the gallery was near where they all lived, they'd come there on foot. They decided to eat somewhere on the way back. Before them a hill rose abruptly, encircled by old terraces of once-fashionable houses, now offices staring sightlessly through their plate-glass windows.

They climbed the long steps that connected the terraces for pedestrians under the shadow of a tall church on the top whose elegant tower defined the city's western skyline. The restaurant was just below it, entered through a basement with a red and white striped awning, a name in French written on it.

When they came out it was late. They'd all had a lot to drink. His friends' flat was near and they insisted he come up.

The drawing-room looked over the park. It was in half-darkness. They left the curtains unpulled. He sat on a big white sofa beside her. Phillip lay at their feet and opened more wine.

He could see the tops of the trees nodding peacefully in the park. He passed the cigarette back to her. It seemed to him that he could reach out and steady the turning room if he wanted to.

I feel as if it was all just, Lindsay exclaimed and then faltered. At this moment. Just right as it is.

Exactly like this, he said.

She leaned back and stretched so that one hand brushed his arm. She smiled.

Tired? he asked, taking her cool hand in both of his.

Mmmm. Not tired exactly. Languorous.

That's how I feel. As if I couldn't move.

Why should you?

Yes, why should you? Phillip mumbled drowsily from the floor. Plenty of room here.

Then that's settled, she said.

Phillip poured them all more wine.

Lindsay was about the same age as him. Perhaps a little older. Phillip was a few years younger than her. She was slim with delicate, somewhat scowling features that he found rather piquant, imagining her frowning as she came. He had never fucked her. The occasion had never arisen.

The room was almost dark now except for the moonlight.

This, he said. All this.

What, Lindsay asked.

He waved his cigarette. She giggled and he laughed.

Good shit, said Phillip solemnly from the floor.

Anything better, he asked.

Yes, they had something better.

And so later.

So later he listened to his own voice telling them something he didn't understand. The tones of his voice seemed beautiful. The timbre. He said a word: *Retinue*. He repeated it: *with his retinue of mediocrities*. That last word exploded in his mouth, the sounds hurtling against his teeth. *Telling continually trailing his retinue of mediocrities*. He tried it again: *Telling with his retinue of mediocrities continually trailing behind him.*

The others weren't listening. Phillip was humming in harmony with the record. He wanted them to know what he felt just then.

Lindsay's hand moved on his arm. When she spoke her voice seemed to wake him though he hadn't been asleep.

We should be in bed by now.

He saw the cigarette glowing red for a long long space of time. Then Phillip passed it up to him.

Lindsay's voice came again as if accompanying a rhythm they had all heard and would not interrupt.

But I'm too lazy even to take my clothes off. And Phillip's too drunk to be any use.

I can give you a little help, he said, moving closer to her.

She put her hand on the top of his thigh.

Can you? she said, smiling at him with her eyes closed. That would be good of you.

He reached towards her and started undoing the buttons of her blouse. She wasn't wearing anything beneath it. When he'd unbuttoned it to the waist they looked at each other for a moment. Then he slowly pulled the blouse aside to reveal her breasts. They were small and firm, as he had expected. He slipped the blouse free of her shoulders.

How kind you are, she said. How can I thank you.

She started to undo his shirt. When they were both naked they stood up. She nudged Phillip with her foot.

Come on. You're not going to bed like that, are you?

He smiled up at them a little drunkenly. They helped him to get to his feet and remove his clothes.

She took him by the hand and began to lead him towards the door. He reached back for Phillip's hand and they both followed her along the corridor.

When they were on the bed he said:

Who do you want to fuck you first?

Guests before family, she replied primly, crouching on the edge.

With his thighs pressed to the back of hers, he cautiously pushed into her, then rocked backwards and forwards while he brushed the tips of her breasts with his fingers. After a moment he felt Phillip's hand on the back of his groin gently easing him in and out of her.

The week-ends were the worst. Especially the afternoons. I hated the silence. Hated worse the muted sounds in the near distance: the passing traffic hurrying to somewhere. Or music from another room, the wailing note of the singer distracting me but the bass not audible.

Tonight he stood at the window in the centre of the front room and looked due west.

The sun was setting in a deep yellow haze, streaked with the black of the clouds, that glowed as if it were a misted glass covering a reddish light.

The room grew dark. Holding his wine-bottle, he walked up the long wide road that led north, and which, lined with tall soot-darkened tenements, still retained the winding form that it had when it was a lane across fields little more than a century ago. Up some of the side-streets tram-rails were still embedded in the cobbles.

Young boys with ill-made dummies propped drunkenly against the railings held out their hands. A man stood in a shop doorway with his back to the road. From his shoes a stream ran across the pavement towards the gutter. Two girls approached giggling, arm-in-arm and supporting each other, stumbling occasionally.

Much of it he was familiar with now. The old men with hands eagerly held out, past whom he walked now. The sullen youths who looked through him. The joylessness. The despair. Or occasionally its opposite that meant the same. Once a red-headed prostitute of sixty singing on the bus, standing at the front and turned back to face the passengers, oblivious of their disapproval, roaring out her rebel songs as she drummed on her thighs, exultantly urging them to sing the chorus.

He turned into another street. Over the railings beside one of the tenements, his eye was suddenly attracted by the abrupt spider-like movement of something black and large that scuttled mechanically into the shadows.

As he reached the close-mouth he was looking for, he heard loud noises coming from one of the flats. He knocked and waited for the door to be opened.

CHAPTER SIX

WATCHING FROM AN opposite corner he saw them at last come in, and pushed through the crush holding the drinks he had bought already.

The beer was cool and flat. It was a distraction from it to have to talk. He had nothing to say that he hadn't said a hundred times before. Lorna's friend said he was giving up his job. He was bored. He hadn't found another.

It wasn't clear why he should care. He looked at the others and reflected on the strangeness of these divided splinters of consciousness, each struggling, suffering, trying to articulate their lives in interesting banalities to ward off the terror and postpone the night. He wanted to tell them that they were squandering their lives in trivialities, but when he began to approach the point he caught a look of fear on their faces and desisted.

While Lorna's friend was getting another round she said:

He won't, you know. He's been saying it for years.

He nodded.

The place was, impossibly, becoming more crowded. It

was getting difficult to hear one another. The low ceiling seemed to mirror the surrounding roar back at them. They were being pushed closer to each other.

He inhaled sharply so that the smoke rasped his throat. His arms, holding beer and cigarette, were being forced to his sides. He glanced round. He noticed a girl alone at the bar. Blonde. Quite young.

She was still there later. On the way back from the toilet he offered to buy her a drink.

I'm waiting on my friend, she said and looked away.

When the other two told him they'd seen him, he explained that intimacy with strangers was the most exciting thing he knew.

He went to get another round.

Still waiting, he said.

Isn't that Gordon Something, that guy you're with?

He told her it was and she let him pay for her drink and went back with him.

I've found a friend of yours, he said.

Gordon merely nodded at her. His hair was receding. He looked worried. It seemed obvious that he had no idea who she was. Luckily it was near closing-time.

When they flashed the lights, Gordon said:

Can we offer you a lift? We're going back West.

He accepted. The girl hesitated, then said yes.

He sat with his arm around her. Jane or Jean. The car was so small she could not object. But when he whispered into her ear, she pretended not to catch his words. The car kept stopping at red lights.

Just drop me off at the corner, he said.

Lorna said:

Aren't you coming back? We thought we'd pick up a couple of curries.

No, not tonight.

The car slowed down.

Will you come up for a coffee or something? he whispered.

She shook her head without looking at him.

Just for half an hour.

But she refused.

Give me your phone number.

No, I won't, she said aloud.

He got out and slammed the door hard.

When he got into bed he became aware of the slope of the floor. It had dropped away so far that when the door was opened it swung several inches above the carpet. Though hardly noticeable by day, this became unignorable when he was in bed. He would lie awake in fear of the building collapsing, for that part of the city was honey-combed by old mine-workings. In many places the road-surface sagged and occasionally a fissure opened suddenly as a tunnel-roof collapsed hundreds of feet underground. Recently a tenement on the edge of the river had slid towards the bank sending diners fleeing in panic from a restaurant on the ground-floor.

The third time it rang he picked it up. After a moment's silence she said:

Why didn't you ring?

I've been busy.

When am I going to see you again?

He paused as if considering.

This week's completely out.

Then when?

Why don't I ring you sometime?

There was a click and then he heard the dialling tone.

As the daylight retreated the bar after work became a refuge which his colleagues were increasingly reluctant to desert for the cold streets.

He moved quickly from one pocket of warmth to another of those dotted around that part of the city. The buses that laboured past him as he walked to and from work were illuminated now, the darkness lifting that late, returning so early.

Once he passed the girl from the gallery cycling towards him as he walked home. He raised his hand but if she even saw him she didn't acknowledge his gesture.

In this city everything was old but nothing was very old – apart from the deconsecrated cathedral that stood at the top of the High Street a mile to the east of where the centre was now. He grew accustomed to the must of old buildings – in the theatres, the cafes, and discos converted from warehouses or churches. What had been one of the world's great ports and before that a citadel of religious fanaticism had declined. Here he was aware of the past as he had not been in more ancient cities he had lived in.

Quite often at that time Paul would lean across his desk and say:

Do you want to make a hit?

He would answer:

Do I want to be rich?

He would follow him to the landing.

Once Magnus came out of the toilet as they went in and looked at them curiously.

I remember what gave me the high I wanted then. I recall the reech of perfume and gin, the jerking rhythm and the way my sweat dropped on to them. And the blow, always the blow.

I remember still the bodies of some of them – Barby's small hard breasts and flat belly, Anna's neck, Cindy's boy-slender thighs. Soft hair falling across my chest, faces contorted in pleasure.

Then the glare of the lamp suddenly on the white

sheets. My head hurting. The buses changing gear outside.

The frightened face, whited, clown-like with its gollywog frizz reappears from the invisibleness of the black background as it moves across the spotlight again. In the silence the feet are heard slapping on the wooden boards. A splatter of cymbals. Another figure appears, boy-girl slim in one-piece tights – its gender erotically indeterminable. It speaks in a voice that leaves the mystery unresolved. Around him the audience laughs at lines he still can't catch.

He glances at the girl beside him. She is leaning forward eagerly. He foresees that he will take her home, that they'll talk, then touch. He intends to stroke the back of his hand down from her bare shoulder towards her breast.

He feels a faint suffusion of desire and wonders if she will consent to the intimacies he plans.

CHAPTER SEVEN

HE'D DRUNK THE wine they'd brought. Tangy. Slightly oaken. Someone had brought a quarter-bottle of vodka and he'd had most of that too. Now he jerked his body to the music, determined to enjoy himself whatever the bitch did.

You *told* me that you *loved* me
As the *sun* sank in the *Bay*!

Mairi swayed, eyes half-shut, creating a zone from which he was excluded, occasionally turning her back to him as if the music so required. When he closed his eyes showers of golden leaves cascaded past him. He subordinated his mind and body to the imperative of the rhythm blasted out by the speakers, alert even to the movement of the floor, as it vibrated to the same beat, stretched between the joists taut like a drum-skin.

He didn't know how long he had been dancing. His shirt was sticking to him. He needed a drink or something.

Fancy going back to the kitchen? he said, having to shout in her ear.

Please yourself.

Before he'd even moved away she started dancing with another couple.

I *didn*'t *know* you *lied* to me
Till *just* the other *day*.

In the hall people were talking in groups. As far as he could tell, nobody was doing anything. At the door he paused as if waiting for someone to come out. Near him a thin girl in a sweater and jeans said:

Lucy said the same happened to her.

A burly man with a thick moustache said:

She should know. Christ, she should know.

You can hold things down, but they rise to the surface once you let go, the girl said.

He crossed to the kitchen and then he saw her. Alone? No. Listening on the edge of a group. Detached but intent. She noticed him looking at her and lowered her eyes. Those thick dark eye-lashes.

He went up to her.

Do you remember me?

She seemed amused.

Didn't you come into the gallery recently?

That's right.

I noticed you earlier.

You should have come over. I've only just seen you.

She smiled slightly and turned away.

Let me get you a drink.

When she turned back she was still smiling.

I must find my friend, she said. We're going now.

Won't you stay for a moment now that I've found you?

At last she looked at him, standing with her legs planted firmly apart. She said:

Shouldn't you get back to your friend?

She doesn't matter, he said.

She turned away again.

Don't go yet. I still don't know your name.

Isn't that a coincidence, she said over her shoulder. I don't know yours.

He overtook her and blocked the doorway.

Come out with me.

She seemed to be inspecting his face.

I'm flattered, she said. But I'm not interested.

Why not?

She thrust her jaw upwards and said:

I don't have any room in my life. Or, to be more precise, I don't choose to make any.

He stepped aside to let her pass. He watched her leave. Her friend was the girl in jeans.

When he went back, Mairi was dancing with another man. He left without telling her he was going.

He said to him:

It's the system. It's not the concept, it's the implementation.

Magnus nodded.

When he saw that he was not going to speak, he said:

The concept's fine, Magnus. I've no worries about the concept.

Magnus's office smelt of wood. He never saw him and Lena socially now. They hadn't, as he had expected, become friends.

Now he said:

I need more time. Does Telling understand that?

Magnus nodded again.

Her face came to obsess him. The long features, pale against the dark sky of her hair. The deep, blue pools and the black fringes that descended to veil them. It seemed to him that she was the centre around which the things that had long puzzled him would form a pattern. Her accent, though faint, was of the city, he believed.

He made his way home through the silent streets uneventfully. When he looked up at the sky it appeared to wheel above him as if he were suddenly aware of the earth revolving at speed.

Sometimes he was wakened by a sharp crack. He would start up in terror, thinking the masonry had sheared, that the building was falling. Yet even in his panic he knew it was not so.

One morning he found that a pile of books and papers he had stacked up the night before had slipped. Evidence, he was sure, of the building's instability.

In contrast to the harshness of the white tiles, the gentle hushing of the pipes was like an animal resting.

This he needed. This calmed him, gave him perspective. In this viewless room, soap-scented, air-warmed, how often had he sat, head hung down, waiting in the opulent silence for the floor to come to rest.

Or – also in this sacred space – Paul fumbling with his bits of silver-paper.

She squeezed the sponge over his head and laughed at his expression of surprise. He moved his foot forward in a pretend kick at her thigh. She seized it and began to tickle it. The water was tepid now, and he noticed how dirty it was. Also that her legs seen from this perspective were too short and plump. She had started soaping his chest, giggling loudly.

Oh I love your chest!

Sshh! he said. People are asleep.

There's no one can hear, she said.

She clutched him with one hand and went on soaping him with the other, bringing her face nearer.

It's so lovely and hairy. Oh, I do love it. I do love you.

She waddled forward on her thighs. He wriggled backwards so that one of the taps rammed his spine.

What's the matter? she said. Are you afraid I've got something smittle?

She leaned forward again, her toddler-fat belly emerging from the water.

Didn't stop you earlier.

He put out a hand and it collided with a swinging breast. She seized it and placed it where she was still wet from the bath. Her face was against his, her hands caressing his nipple and stomach.

Oh darling! Darling!

That was what she had cried out earlier in the ecstasy of her climax. He wondered what he was doing here. This room was the inner sanctum of a religion where he could not worship: the thick carpeting, the fluffy tea-cosy round the pedestal, the cluster of bottles on the glass shelf, the bright childish colours of the expensive fabrics and fittings. The barbarous accoutrements – not mysterious but alienating – of a threatening femaleness. He yearned suddenly for his own city.

But had she really forgotten his name or was she pretending?

She screamed.

She screamed when he fucked her. Squealed. She made him use a sheath because she didn't like his stuff inside her.

Sshh, he said again.

First Paul or Willi fumbling. Then the rush, the hit, the surge, the acceleration like a powerful car roaring away from lights or better like a jet angling – thrusting straight at the sky, so that he wanted to shout, this is it, this is being alive.

Hugging Paul's hands whose face, suddenly pale and complex, smiles back.

So the darkness, so the days. So the not-thinkingness, the hand sliding over a thigh in not-knowingness as the darkness came earlier each day and he, returning each night cat-conscious on the unlit streets, felt that if he looked up at the tall buildings on either side between which he stole he would see them meeting far over his head.

Dreams.

The city from the top of a high building surrounded by similar towers, each belching plumes of thick smoke, and between them the narrow streets and parks laid out like a toy-town. He feeling exultation mingled with regret.

Or fleeing across fields. A cross-country race of his schooldays but now his pursuers were going to kill him. Fording a river, the mud sticking to his feet. His legs moving unavailingly. Suddenly, the edge of a cliff – a dizzying drop and the long long fall into terrified wakefulness.

Her. Where in the city? Near, he knew. When he passed the gallery he averted his gaze, hurried ahead. Approaching cyclists he eyed warily, unsure of what to do if. But never.

And he searched. On hands and knees, his nose furrowing in the darkness of hard hair, wiry, warm moistness. Tongue curving into cunt-lips, fingers further.

The pleasure began from the moment the eyes rested on

the bosom, the crotch. Encounters everywhere. The street, pubs, buses. Trains especially. Where they sat, knees pointed, as if waiting for a religious service to begin. He, ready to worship the mysteries they pressed between their thighs, pressing leg against bare knee. Or when, thrown against each other by the carriage yawing violently from side to side, names, perhaps numbers, exchanged.

Approaching its height later when the hand moved towards the thigh, the hunter's sense of smell alerted to detect signs of fear. The moment of delicious uncertainty and the peak – the first token of surrender, of hand moving towards buckle or button. And the roughness of metal or leather on bare skin, the slow unveiling of vulnerability, a girl's breasts her shy admission of desire. Then her cool hands on his own body, fingers brushing as if by accident against his red swelling, the roughness of his thighs against her smooth skin.

And the sweet certainty of slipping in, of a welcome where nothing is forced. A tug-of-war where each wants the other to keep the game going, not end it. And at the moment of coming, clarity reduced to this point, this part, all meaning held by these motions.

But then the consequence: nothing resolved.

The cycle resumes.

CHAPTER EIGHT

THE COUNTRY, THOUGH the language was almost his own, remained mysterious. Its bleak landscape – the taciturn record of its bloody history – conveyed little to him. The ancient capital – to which his work took him occasionally – with the castle crouched high above the narrow wynds and steep streets, moved him by its beauty but seemed wholly foreign.

The abrasive intimacies of the city's street-life he found exciting, but he missed the defensive reticence of his own slower-spoken countrymen. Often he was woken by cries of pain or rage in the street.

Magnus explained it to them:

He took a down. A big one. Telling wouldn't give him another chance.

Another chance? Paul asked.

A second chance. You're not allowed even one mistake. You have to keep your head above water all the time.

Afterwards, when Magnus had left the pub, Paul said:

He was hitting too much. He was bound to get caught.

So he's gone?

Straight away. Security escorted him up to empty his desk and then took him to the door. He was asking for it, though. He went too long.

Willi hadn't been a particular friend of his, but he would miss him.

He had met Joanne quite recently. She had a warm flat a few minutes' walk from his own. She was plain and older than him but her body was slender, her arse slim, her breasts pointed and firm and she loved to fuck. It gave them both pleasure for him to straddle her on the thick white rug in front of an open fire, the long pile soft on his legs and the heat warming his sides while the hi-fi murmured and Sylvester dozed a few feet away. He liked it that she knew he only wanted to see her when there was no one else to fuck.

He rang her from work and came round after. She cooked for him – she cooked well. He bought wine on the way and they talked and drank. He enjoyed talking to her almost as much as he enjoyed fucking her. Then they fucked.

Sylvester watched, his eyes invisible until they opened briefly – glittering honey deep in the black.

The rain descended unhurriedly. There was a dull pain at the back of his head, but in spite of it he had worked most of the morning. The papers, which he had bought when he walked the girl from last night to the taxi-rank, failed to hold his interest. The concerts and plays they described were too far away. He had no time to read the books reviewed. From the next close came a muted thudding which he did not hear but felt, while above it a voice rose and fell.

He stood at the window. Even with the cold and the rain, the emptiness and quiet were mysterious. He felt too unwell to start working again and too restless to do nothing. His year here would turn into two, he intended. But no more. The city's sense of a separate destiny interested him, but he felt excluded from it.

The trees in the park opposite were almost motionless as if holding their branches steady to cup the rain. It was cold, but even so he was surprised to see snow, now melting in the rain, on the roof of a car parked in the street below. It must have come from the mountains.

Now the rain had stopped. He watched people going into the park. Two figures caught his attention. A young woman and a small child.

In the interval between showers he walked slowly along a gravelled path. To his right, further down the slope, the child was running up and down on the grass picking up and scattering handfuls of wet leaves. The body, further rounded out by warm clothes and a woollen hat, had still almost the shape of a baby. The mother was watching from the lower path.

Near him the child fell suddenly. A moment's astonishment, perhaps at the proximity of the wet-smelling grass, then it started to scream. He moved forward quickly and raised it by its upper arms. The contorted face, interrupted by this unforeseen intervention, expressed uncertainty whether to smile or cry.

Kneeling, oblivious of the damp, he coaxed the child, still holding its body, the miniature gum-booted feet declining to take the weight. The blue eyes, though smaller and darker, were familiar, especially in their quality of considered surprise. Behind the shoulders which he gripped he saw the high-pitched roofs and lattice-worked spire, black against the grey sky, of the university. The tears were withheld, he thought, not because his efforts were successful, but only by amazement at his ineptness.

The child's eyes focused on something behind him and a shadow fell. He did not look up. She stooped beside him, squatting more elegantly than he knelt, to protect her skirt from the grass, and seconded his blundering attempts to soothe. So they worked together, she as if unsurprised that it was him. He yielded to her expertise.

Nice man, she comforted. Say hello to David.

A mittened hand was held out to him and he squeezed it cautiously. The adults straightened and a brief conspirators' smile passed between them. He needed to do or say nothing. In a moment they walked on together, holding the child between them.

The cessation of the rain and now the apparition of a little blue had wrought its effect: there were other people in the park. As they rounded the hill they saw the southern expanse of the city, the rows of high-arched necks that marked the docks, and the great estuary glittering in the distance, while in a wide ring around the horizon ran the bruise-coloured line of distant hills.

She told him her name was Lucy. He felt she could have had no other.

Though this was a fine example, they agreed on a dislike of parks. Zoos, he suggested, where wild country was caged and exhibited. She smiled as if in enjoyment of the idea, but at its whimsicality too. She wore a long dark coat that accentuated her height and slimness, the blackness of her hair and her pale face.

The path had brought them back in a leisurely circle.

I live just over there, he explained, pointing over the tops of the trees. He but not she knew that his windows were just visible. He told her the address but when the trees rustled suddenly and the rain started again he did not ask her and the child to shelter there. As they ran towards one gate he returned home by another.

Their encounter had been inevitable, it seemed to him, and he felt no guilt for having manipulated both her and events. He had not fingered the bloom of chance. Or if fingered, then only slightly. She had accepted him as if acknowledging some right he possessed. As he thought about her now, he became aware with amazement that he wanted more than merely her body.

He walked cautiously along the slippery pavement, and across the shiny road where the traffic was still desultory.

So she had remembered his name.

In his own street the oblong paving stones gripped better, each straight but curving to contribute its little portion of the earth's circumference. And beneath the cusped stones – gravel earth rock – but wormed by mine-working. He placed his feet on a thin crust, aware of the dark vacuities far below.

CHAPTER NINE

THE RIVER WAS between them. He crossed the bridge. Her street was halfway up the hill – tall old buildings blackened by much more than a century of the city's atmosphere. Except that on the side opposite her flat, scaffolding had been erected for stone-cleaning. There were lamps hung from the ends of the poles to warn drivers and pedestrians. Her flat occupied the top two floors.

She led him through the hall and up a narrow flight of stairs, then unlocked a door at the top. In the near-darkness he smelt paint. She turned on a small bedside lamp and by its dim light he could see that he was in a huge room with a high ceiling and a big skylight. There was an easel, and canvases stacked against the wall.

They sat on cushions on the thin carpet leaning back against a mattress pushed up against the wall, holding their mugs of coffee, her long legs stretched out alongside his. She smiled as if at some secret source of amusement. A record was playing.

Afterwards, he remembered their conversation very

clearly. He spoke with diffidence, aware that this was unusual for him. She asked him where he was from, about his work, about his plans. She wanted to know, and yet asking him seemed to be a kind of game.

His work was interesting. And exciting, for much of it was being done for the first time. He was lucky to be involved in it. There were other countries he could go to, he told her. Once his project here was completed. He saw himself on an autobahn, the rain splashing on the windscreen, the wipers working furiously, headlights flashing towards and past him. He suddenly perceived his future as an artefact, his career as something he could make. The corners of the vast room receded into shadow. It was getting cold. He knew it must be very late.

He moved his hand towards her. She placed hers over it. Except that he didn't want to speak, he would have asked her what the music was. In its plangency more poignant and beautiful than any experience was likely to be. Unless this lingered in the memory as a moment of sweetness enfolded in the darkness.

He turned. Beneath their dark lashes the blue eyes, clearer than any he had seen, were on him. There was no secret joke now. Her scrutiny was completely serious. He had never looked into a woman's face in that way before, so long and hard. Always an evasion by kiss or smile had protected him. Her gaze was not inquisitorial but inquisitive. He believed he was being tested, sounded. He didn't understand why, but he felt unable to touch her.

He spoke slowly as if drugged:

I must go. It's after midnight.

Her unveiled gaze registered a change. Surprise? Amusement? Hurt?

You don't have to go, she said. Why don't you stay here?

With an odd explicitness, she half-turned her head towards the mattress. Then as if to make quite clear what she meant, she said very simply, almost like a child:

It's my bed.

A moment later she put her hand on his shoulder and asked:

Why are you crying?

Then she furrowed her brow in an expression of mock-suspicion and said:

Or are you laughing?

And now he was.

He gripped her slender neck with one hand stroking with the other her head so delicately shaped, smoothing back the soft hair that fell over her ears, to disclose the pale lobes on which he tenderly closed his teeth. When he stroked her she unfolded like a flower – such sweetness, such pleasure.

He felt he was nosing into harbour, to berth between her slender thighs. As if he brought to her his frailties stored by day, offered to her balm by night. And she too, for when she clutched him she cried out and pressed him to her like a plaster to stanch a wound.

His cock in her felt like a plug, a cork, by which he made her safe, pushing gently against her, his fingers moving towards another opening into her body.

What would it mean to say that I loved her? That I was fixated on her? That she gave me a high, the biggest turn-on I'd known? That she was the first woman that I cared if anything bad happened to her? That I didn't feel self-conscious when I was with her? That being with her was as untroubling as being alone – only a lot nicer?

He saw Magnus rarely now. Once when he went with him to a nearby bar they found Paul there. He was with Peter and seemed pleased to see them. Peter asked why he never saw him in the canteen.

I usually skip lunch.

Peter made a face:

You don't want to start that caper. You've got to give yourself breaks, otherwise this job's a killer.

Paul nodded and said:

What are you trying to hold down? Let it go. Let it rise.

Magnus sipped his beer watchfully. It was cold and sharp like a knife-blade in the guts. After a few pints they went to a curry-house.

CHAPTER TEN

THE SNOW, NOT cleared from the pavements, was stamped down and froze hard. The hill between them, ungritted, was a hazard difficult of negotiation.

The studio was vast and cold. Only in her bed were they warm. They slept on the mattress laid down in a corner. The smell of paint irritated his nose. And often as he climbed to her flat he was assailed on the stair by a rank smell from the flats below. Both toilets and kitchens had vents on to the landings and he could not tell which was the source of the gut-intimate, earth-innards-shit stench.

In the middle of the night they woke up. Once awake, the room was painfully cold. They talked. She was curious to know what he made of the city. She had come there when she married. She told him nothing about her life before she met him.

In the middle of the night the mind floats free as if intoxicated.

He told her once:

I don't like my friends.

She laughed, pretending to stuff a sheet into her mouth to stop herself.

I really don't. It's not just that they bore me, but most of them offend me too.

Well *I* like my friends.

He held her thin arm. He wasn't sure if he had slept. She was breathing evenly but he thought she was awake. He had met none of her friends, though he had heard her mention a Jane and a Kate. Her life apart from himself was mysterious.

They had come in late and got into bed in the dark. The curtains were left undrawn. He saw the astonishing mist of stars through the skylight. She asked him softly if he was awake and he told her that when he learned at school that the earth was spinning he became terrified of being flung off if he stopped concentrating.

She rested her dark head against his chest and he heard her breathing grow deeper and more regular.

He stubbed out that cigarette too and stamped his feet. He rested one hand on the railing at the top of the steps. Even through the glove he could feel it burn. He watched his breath hang white in the air and then dissolve.

At last a group came out. Both boys and girls lavishly made up, their hair dyed and cut in the season's – next season's? – fashion. The defiantly ugly elegance of their clothes gave them in a group a slightly menacing air, absent when they were encountered on their own.

He saw her before she found him, carrying, like most of them, a large portfolio. The others so young, she looked no older. Why should she separate from the group and come to him? He saw her glance round for him and then – deliberately to provoke him? – turn back to her friends.

But at last she came to him.

Had she thought about him at all that morning?

She lowered her head and turned away. When she let him see her face she was grinning mischievously. The restaurant was nearby. As they walked away he noticed Alison watching them. Her round face sad and inquisitive.

The city changed for him now. He woke from the trance which his daily life had become.

Buying a packet of butter he wondered at the squareness of the hard shiny brick, the beauty of the foil dappled with water-drops. Noticed for the first time the woman who sold him his newspaper.

How had he missed so much? How had he never noticed the elaborate glass, the profusion of exuberant tiling on close-walls, the delicate plaster-work tracery on ceilings in the big rooms left lit with the curtains drawn back?

This city, so far from anywhere, so brutalized by history that its citizens clawed for things of beauty, now seemed to him a Florence turned inside out – the great tenements palaces whose best artefacts were all on display.

All this he savoured as he traversed the elegant streets that climbed the hills which rose and fell like the backs of knobbled fingers.

These streets were criss-crossed now by invisible ley lines: the ways between his flat and hers, the gallery, the school, their restaurants.

Looking at her across the table he wondered if she was happy. Her smile was secretive, perhaps forced or automatic. He knew little of her previous lovers. Of the child's father – her husband? – he knew nothing.

Once she said, There's so much you don't know about me. She had been regretting it as an inevitability, not offering to remedy it.

Now he said to her: Who is Leven?

Her eyes became suddenly watchful or playful.

Had there been anything?

She smiled.

They paused while the waiter placed their fragrant bhajees in front of them.

This *is* a treat, she said, seizing a piece and dousing it in the green sauce. I don't usually eat at this time.

She explained to him who Leven was.

The game required that he press further.

Did she find him attractive?

Eyes lowered to her plate, in a small voice as if reluctantly confessing:

Yes, she did, she said.

So?

She was leaning forward. As she gazed at him the solemnity of her features was undermined by a look in the eyes. Suddenly he felt something on his thigh. Her face stared back at him but her head grew lower and now he felt his zip being undone.

On the floor below were the kitchen, Alison's room, the sitting-room they shared, and the child's bedroom. The studio covered the full width of the building, and the roof was high. Its big skylight made it very cold.

They crouched before the open fire in the corner where she slept. Her hair smelt of coal as if its blackness derived from that subterranean mineral, and it shone like coal when it caught the light. Against her hair the skin was very pale. He watched her as she slept.

Making love her face became even younger, nun-like, rapt in its devotedness, her mouth held a little open, her nostrils dilating very slightly. She never smiled, stared at him in unrecognizing surprise. Climaxing, her eyes opened and shut quickly, the lashes brushing his cheekbone like a trapped moth beating its wings.

Telling's secretary rang down to make an appointment.

His office had one wall of plate-glass through which the city looked like a vast photograph – motionless at this remove. Far away was a line of bright lights that marked the airport. He talked for a long time, but the drift of what he was saying was difficult to catch. At intervals he paused, but not as if he was inviting comment. When at last he spoke about the contract it was difficult to know if he was pleased or concerned.

He became aware of movement. When he was fully awake he saw that she was tossing restlessly. Her eyes opened briefly disclosing glimpses of startled blue. She began to sob, her cheeks flat and pale but her nose reddening.

He touched her arm and she started away, staring back at him through a curtain of hair. He spoke her name over and over again until at last she allowed him to touch her.

He held her and rocked her. Like a small child she muttered through her sobs:

I'm no good.

Silly girl. Silly silly girl.

I'm no good. I deserve to die.

He leaned on to her and whispered into her ear:

I love you. I love you.

The words shocked him but she registered no impression.

At last she drifted back to sleep and he followed her into unconsciousness.

She was from the capital, he learned, but her accent was so slight that he was not surprised to have been wrong.

He went to her whenever she would let him and they

both were free. He felt he was feeding off her energy and wondered if she felt that and resented it.

She would kiss him suddenly like a little girl and then giggle and try to get away when he held her so that they would struggle together. Then he would whisper into her ear the thing he wanted to do to her and she would suddenly put her arms round him and breathe: Is that a promise?

Until then, he believed, he'd never made love. Never known the finding of self in the unawareness of self, the celebration of something beyond the pleasure of receiving – even of giving – delight through the intimacy of two strangers' bodies.

The people of the city appeared to have a concerted purpose – to pass their lives in the cold and rain and greyness with as little mutual abrasiveness as possible. Existences of great privacy were being lived, and venturing on to the streets was only a means to that end. The city was a complicated mechanism for avoiding human contact, it once occurred to him.

As winter advanced the streets along which he hurried became deep alleyways for the wind and rain to hurtle through. He became increasingly reluctant to leave the warmth of his bed or hers in the flesh-scraping cold of the mornings.

They were both working hard. It was difficult for them

to meet more than once or twice a week. When they went out Alison usually looked after the child. Because they were both tired they talked about a week-end break away from the city, but he didn't believe it would happen.

His curiosity about her past increased. Was she married? Who was the child's father? Did she still see him? All these questions she parried and, unwilling to invade, he desisted.

Was there something wrong with the child? he wondered. It always looked sickly. And it rarely spoke. But he knew nothing about children.

She said again:

I was hoping you'd ring.

When he didn't answer she said:

It's been a long time. I wondered if everything's all right.

Fine, he said. I've been very busy.

She said:

Do you want to arrange something?

Look Joanne, let me ring you when I get my head above water.

He put the receiver down wondering how long she would wait.

Against the raw cold they lay under the covers in the near-darkness, their gaze towards the end of the mattress, her hand holding him, squeezing or stroking to keep him hard, his fingers pleasuring her, occasionally turning to nibble each other, the blue-grey shadows frequently left to whisper together unregarded in the corners of the room.

Once she said:

Leven was here this afternoon.

He said:

Did anything happen?

Delightedly she said:

What do you mean?

He ran the back of one finger over a nipple that was showing over the cover. It hardened.

She sighed:

He's never shown any interest in me that way.

And if he did?

She smiled.

Though he knew she couldn't respond – knew that her attempt to say the right things would annoy him – he told her:

We lost nearly six hundred.

They were in a restaurant. The other tables were empty.

Lost?

Lost track of it. Not *lost* it for Chrissake. He laughed. Lost the use of it for nearly seven hours. So we dropped a three.

How? Whose fault was it?

He shrugged.

No, tell me, she said. I'm interested. Try to explain it.

These things happen.

Is it bad?

It doesn't help. Telling wasn't too happy.

Three? she said. You mean, three thousand?

He shook his head.

Hundred thousand?

He shook his head again.

She said:

Whose fault was it?

You can't say it's anyone's fault. It's a system failure.

The startled quality in her eyes continued to astonish him. Waking beside her he would turn warily towards the dazzle of the blue, timid of their demand. Fires extinguished by the white lids like candle-snuffers. But only in sleep when her face became a small child's, even to the fist screwed into the mouth. After she had slept in his bed he would find tufts from her woolly black shirt that she often kept on, and would brush them out in the morning, like the spoor of some exotic creature.

She refused to see him as often as he wanted. Several times she failed to show up when they had agreed to meet. She never explained or apologized or admitted she had been wrong. This provoked and attracted him. If he tried to reproach her she either smiled and said nothing or snapped at him.

They met only after dark, parted before dawn now that the winter solstice was almost upon them.

She slept badly, muttered in her sleep. Once she called out and woke him. She drove her head against the pillow. Let me go, let me go. Her eyes open but unseeing.

Sometimes she rang him to cancel a meeting. Rang off if he protested. Or arrived late and refused to explain. He had to learn not to examine her. Not to notice. Darkness under the eyes. That sweet face that shied away from him when he reached out. Don't touch me.

He rocked backwards and forwards, feeling himself jammed.

It was strange to be in the town on a week-day afternoon. When he got to the right building he followed her directions and found the exhibition-room. He saw her talking to some people he didn't know. She noticed him and after a few minutes she came over. When she reached him she didn't hold up her face to be kissed.

What's the matter?

There are people watching.

Who cares.

He kissed her and she reddened.

Which are yours?

She pointed. He went over.

Oh yes, I like them.

She walked along the line.

You've seen that one before, and that one. But not that one.

They all looked the same to him and he was afraid he had been tactless, but then he realized she wasn't interested in his feelings about them. Here, as perhaps elsewhere for her, his judgement counted for nothing.

As he watched her looking at the paintings, considering them with extraordinary seriousness as if seeing them for the first time, he felt her utter remoteness from him in her unselfconsciousness – whether of a child or a professional he didn't know. He felt jealous.

I'll bet you're the one they're all talking about.

She turned away. Over her shoulder she said, looking at the next set of canvases:

What do you think of those.

He glanced at them.

They're just second-rate Don Levens. Yours are the best here.

Still with her back to him she said:

Don't patronize me.

CHAPTER ELEVEN

IT WAS THE pressure he was addicted to. The fear. That he could lose so much, so quickly.

He had a bigger office now. Higher. He never pulled the curtains, astonished always by the view straight across the city – especially at night: the undulating strings of yellow lights, the glint of the moon on the river.

He hammered again.

I know you're in there!

He shook the door. Held by a single bolt, it rattled promisingly.

Don't be silly. Alison told me you're in.

There was silence. He bent his head to listen at the door.

It was dark at the top of the little staircase. The smell of Alison's supper drifted up to him. He heard the child's voice addressing questions to her but the replies were too softly spoken to reach him.

Suddenly he said:

Are you all right?

Go away.

Her voice held no trace of humour or good nature.

I want to see you.

I'm working. Go to hell.

Lying in bed at night trying to sleep, he felt as if a nerve were being exposed when a lorry or a night-bus passed along the main road at the end of the street, and he sensed the floor vibrating and heard the windows rattle.

As she straightened up from kneeling to the oven, he told her:

Paul's dead.

She looked at him closely. Her tact creating embarrassment, Alison left the room.

I don't know who he is.

I work with him. I've mentioned him. Often enough, for fuck's sake, he added.

He felt irritation that she wasn't more interested.

People die, she said.

Only three years older than me.

In answer to her question he said:

There was a car accident.

Oh well, she said. Then it was just chance. She turned back to the casserole. Don't worry. You're okay for a while.

No. He wasn't hurt. But then he had a heart-attack.

The truth was that he was hitting too much. Everyone was at that time. But then you couldn't do the job. At least, he couldn't and I thought I couldn't either.

It wasn't the right job for me. Pressure, yes. I've never been afraid of that. But not that amount. Not for that long.

It seemed she was reproaching his self-indulgence.

You don't really care, she said. About *him*.

He conceded this. And yet.

She said:

After all, it's the most natural thing.

At his age? he exclaimed.

At any age.

Her uninterest shocked him. He had had very little experience of death.

His work allowed him few opportunities to see her, so often he came very late, sometimes letting himself into the darkened flat, groping his way through the hall (without putting on the light to avoid disturbing Alison and the child) and up the stairs to get on to the mattress beside her as she slept.

Sometimes he left before she woke up.

She said:

You think it's something I do to fill my spare time, don't you.

No, he said. I know it's important to you.

Important to me but not important. You think what you do's important and what I do is pointless.

Look, I just told you I liked it for Christ's sake.

She lifted it down from the easel. I'll never show you another. I thought it was a mistake.

I told you I liked it. What am I supposed to say.

Frankly I don't give a fuck about your opinion. What do you know about it. Fuck all.

I just said it reminded me of . . .

I know what you said. Then in the voice copied from Thirties movies that she sometimes used, she said: It only shows, my dear, how little you know about it.

I just said what it reminded me of, he said.

His books and papers were being covered in a fine greasy grime. Dirt was coming in through the gaps in the windows. The flat needed attention. He had little time or energy. To invest what he had would be compromising. He wanted no further excuse for attachment to the place.

His bedroom, though smaller, faced east, the direction from which the coldest wind blew. Sometimes he left the fire on while he slept, waking later to find the tiny beads of blue flame bubbling gently.

The cinema was nearby. They walked there almost in silence.

When she arrived he sensed her mood. She took off her

headscarf and shook her head so that the hair showered drops. He saw the aggression.

Depressed, his mind disengaged as they walked the familiar route, he felt himself slip away from where he was, from when. It was as if, involuntarily, he was remembering now from ten, twenty years in the future.

He looked at her. It seemed a kind of treachery. Yet he examined her dispassionately.

She spoke, and with an effort he recalled himself to this moment.

The noises at night were getting worse, and now he had proof that the building was moving. Quite often the toilet-seat refused to stay upright. He was sure that had only started happening recently.

He was shy of the child, wary of a relationship – unused to children anyway, but afraid to be compromised. He saw little of her, for usually she was in bed by the time he came round.

Once he said:

Let's get out into the country. Summer's too long to wait.

She agreed and he knew that the fact that she raised no objection meant that she didn't take it seriously.

I mean it, he said.

He wondered if she thought it pointless to plan for even a few weeks ahead.

His own flat's size, which had once seemed to signal potential, now conveyed menace. A solid wall of cold waited for him when he returned at night. But it hardly mattered since the demands of his work meant that he was there so little.

He prepared meals in a corner of the great kitchen, but often bought pilaus from an Indian restaurant on the way home. Finding hard oval pellets on the table and sideboard, he gradually ceded areas of the kitchen.

In the sitting-room the windows shook as the wind gusted against them. During the evenings and week-ends as he sat working, he was chilled by draughts. He turned the fire full up and it scorched him.

Why did he feel so estranged from her, so lonely, at that moment when, writhing beneath him, covered in sweat, her teeth bared, her arm hit him in the face and she didn't notice?

At the edges of the sticking-plaster he could see the bruise. She said angrily:

I told you, I must have skidded.

But why?

What do you mean, why?

You don't just skid suddenly on . . .

I've told you.

He seized her arm, gripping hard. He said:

For fuck's sake, what is going on?

She wrenched herself away.

Did somebody do this to you?

You're insane. Look at the bloody bicycle if you don't believe me.

Did he do it?

Who are you talking about?

Her father.

You don't know what you're talking about.

She looked surprised when she said it, but he couldn't tell if it was because he had guessed right or because she really didn't know what he meant.

I worked hard.

I can see now, too intensely, lacking the detachment to see the whole. Perhaps Telling and the others were right, though I still think I was treated badly.

They quarrelled about the dangerous things she did.

It maddened him that he had put his happiness at stake by investing it in someone so careless of her own safety. He was haunted by images of accidents. He thought of her delicate head – the skull eggshell thin – that he could cup with one hand, and the slender neck, lying in a gutter bloodied, the hair matting. He resented the fact that she never seemed to think about him when they weren't together. He thought about her all the time. She never rang him. It was always he who contacted her.

He asked her to see him more often.

She considered for a moment and then said simply:

I don't want to.

He argued with her. Eventually she said:

I suppose the truth is that if I really loved you I *would* want to.

She didn't intend it to be so brutal but that made it the more so. He got up from the mattress and started pulling on his clothes.

There was a period when he had to work all night. And once or twice, after Tokyo had closed down, he hurried to her flat.

Lit by the yellow lamps, the streets were like exhibits in some monstrous museum. Few lights were on and he passed nobody in the street. But near her flat, in an upper room that was brightly lit, he saw a tall palm-tree and the broad leaves of tropical plants and wondered what exotic life flowered there.

Each time they quarrelled the thread that tied them together snapped. One or the other had to make the first move. Usually it was he, but this time he held back from ringing her.

Walking about the city he wondered if he would meet her. In their own district the chances seemed high.

Though angry with her, the memories that pressed upon him were all of her smile, her face unaware of his scrutiny, of her beauty.

Instead he kept seeing Paul. He glimpsed his distinctive figure moving quickly ahead of him in the street, or disappearing round a corner, always carrying his bulk with the slightly aggressive swiftness that he remembered.

Dusk was approaching. He had left work early. He sat by the window trying to read, but he kept thinking of what Magnus had said.

Towards the west he saw the pale yellow sky swiftly obscured by a mass of cloud. A gleaming strip remained near the horizon against which the trees of the park were black, trembling rapidly as their topmost branches responded to the wind.

Very late it began to rain. The wind hurled the waterdrops against the windows like handfuls of small pebbles.

When he woke up in the middle of the night the rain was still heavy, though the wind had dropped. The relentlessness of the downpour was reassuring.

When he arrived he thought she would have food ready but she had already eaten.

I'll get a carry-out from the Taj, he said.

No, I'll make you something.

Don't bother.

If you want food you'll get it.

She opened drawers and cupboards violently, banging things down on the sideboard.

I'm afraid it'll all be out of tins, she said.

She seized a tin and went at it fiercely with the opener. He said:

Be careful.

When she started on the second tin the blade jumped and cut into her thumb. She tried to hide it but she had to drop the opener and wrap a cloth round the wound. When he saw the blood he became angry:

You stupid bitch! I told you!

She pretended he wasn't there. The bleeding didn't stop so she held her hand under the tap. He hated her when she behaved as she did now – blocking him out, nullifying him. When he went to help her with the bandage she moved away.

I told you anyway I didn't want your fucking tins.

Awkwardly because of her injury, she picked up each tin and emptied it into the rubbish-bin.

That was stupid, wasn't it.

She went into the hall, indicating that he should follow. She led him down the stairs, opened the door with difficulty and with her uninjured hand held it open for him.

The stench of his own cigarettes, the odour of his body, clung to him even if he showered and changed his clothes several times a day.

Apart from work, he went nowhere. His car sat unused for days outside his flat.

This was the down, he knew. The dark depression that came on so suddenly.

No possible end or goal could justify raising and lowering his feet like this. He would die here in the bare street.

Unless, only, it were easier not to die but to keep walking.

She ate rapidly as if afraid the food would be taken away. Or perhaps that he would leave.

She said:

This is quite a treat.

The place was expensive. He hadn't been there before. He was irritated by her anxiety to please.

Back at her flat she stretched her legs out in front of the fire, her shoes off. Her legs were not long or slender but well-shaped. Athletic. Her skirt was short. He sat beside her on the rug. As they talked she smiled but her eyes were guarded. Sylvester was curled up against the fender at her head.

He ran his hand along the rough nylon from the toes to the knee, where he paused.

She said:

Have you broken up?

He said:

Can I stay?

That girl. That strange girl who works at the gallery. Have you stopped seeing her?

When he made no answer she said:

Yes, of course.

It excited him that she knew he was making use of her.

She smiled, shutting her eyes. Her face rounded. One hand reached towards his chest, slipped between the buttons of his shirt.

I was frightened of her. Or rather for her. Not because of the violence. Not that, because I didn't really see that until much later – although I suppose I should have. No, I was frightened of her for me. Of what she made me feel, the pity and the guilt.

He paused at the crossing seeing the lights of a black vehicle coming very fast along the empty road. Opposite him a man stepped into the road and began to cross. The driver sounded his horn and, confused, the drunk paused. Too late the driver braked and, on the wet surface, the taxi began to skid.

He waited for the thud, unable to avert his gaze from the drunk, hands absurdly held up to shield his face. But the vehicle spun round in a circle and came to rest, stalled, pointing with an air of surprise in the direction it had come from.

He supposed he hadn't said it with a lot of forethought or with the intention of wounding. But that was surely what made it worse. *That's history*. It had just slipped out in the course of the discussion.

And like a fool, he hadn't said anything at the time. And then later – too late – he had tried to defend himself. He had said:

It's not the concept.

He had tried to assert that it was a system-issue. But Magnus had said:

The concept's been tried. It's had it. I've told you, it's history.

And the others looked embarrassed and then Telling brought them back to the agenda.

Every day he walked past men and women and kids holding out their hands and saying, spare us tenpence, mister? It was cold now. Unemployment was increasing. The business pages were full of the subject. It gratified him – and he felt guilty for it – to feel secure and prosperous as he walked past them.

Once inside his flat, the door closed on the world, he felt safe. Security. Yet you were never safe. He thought of Willi.

And that thought created its own pleasure. If the people begging in the street were wholly alien, suffering a fate to which you were immune, then you derived no sense of guilty pleasure from their misery.

The thought that he could lose his job and would have nothing excited him.

CHAPTER TWELVE

WHEN HE RANG she sounded nonchalant. Did she want to see him?

If he liked.

Well, did she or didn't she?

Yes, let's. It seems ages.

How long do you think it is?

It was much longer than she suggested.

You don't seem very keen. Perhaps I won't bother.

As you like, she said.

He hesitated, knowing her pride was as raw as his own.

When she opened the door her manner was distant, even haughty. Without speaking she led him into the kitchen. She offered him coffee and told him to sit down. They sat on opposite sides of the table, not looking at each other.

They spoke about trivialities, until he said suddenly:

I was hoping you'd ring me.

Oh. Were you?

Yes. Why didn't you?

You always used to ring *me*, she said.

He thought her voice quavered. She turned her head away and started sobbing.

I thought you'd stopped caring for me.

He got up and knelt beside her chair. She kept her head averted but he took her arm. He pulled it gently. She resisted but then released it. He stroked it, whispering her name again and again. At last she turned her head. Her nose was red and her long lashes wet with tears.

As he kissed her he felt a mixture of triumph and pain. Something of her mysteriousness had been dissipated. He felt now that they were fated to hurt one another.

He didn't go south for the holiday. He felt he couldn't spare the time. She went back to the capital where she had an aunt, so he worked all through the festivities of the year's end.

It stayed light later but the cold was increasing. The big rooms were indeed difficult to heat. He stuffed newspapers into the cracks around the window-frames, covering his hands with grime. The effect was inelegant and only partially successful.

The woman had got into the car before he realized that it was, that it might be, her.

He was driving down the main road near her house. He saw a man and a woman talking on the opposite side of the street. There was a jam. In the interstices between traffic, through the windows of other cars, he tried to read what was happening. He thought they were smiling and laughing. Or they might have been shouting at each other. Either way, the man seemed to have his hand on her arm. A bus was stalled between him and them so he could not see. When it had gone they were getting into the car. The man seemed to be forcing her. Then they drove quickly away. By the time he had turned his own car he would have lost it.

Often he missed lunch or ate sandwiches at his desk, all afternoon feeling his belly puffed and heavy, looking forward to the first drink of the evening to settle his stomach, though now he usually had to return to his office after a hasty dinner nearby.

It was true that I didn't like my friends. But I never intended to be there very long. I never saw the place as more than a brief stage. Yet I suppose I became quite fond of Joanne. She is someone else I still wonder about.

Magnus opened the door of his office late one evening. With the light behind him his features were almost invisible.

I noticed your light on.

Come in for a minute.

Magnus stayed where he was.

Don't you think you should back off a bit?

How do you mean?

Get out from under. Just ease back a wee bit.

He held the door for a few moments longer and then closed it behind him.

He was viewing a top-floor flat. The old woman who was showing it had lived there for years. As she chattered, he became aware that the three floors below had been demolished so that the flat they were in hung between the buildings on either side of it. Merely the floorboards, the joists, and a layer of lath and plaster beneath. As he realized this he noticed that he was falling. The floor had given way, but as he dropped through space he saw that he had left the bricks and planks of the building behind.

The start with which he thought he hit the ground was the shock of waking.

She said:

I'm not, but anyway, what would it matter if I did? You see other women. Why shouldn't I do it? What does it matter?

Who was he?

I don't know what you're talking about. I get into cars with friends quite often. How can I remember?

It was only ten days ago for Christ's sake.

When she didn't answer he said:

It was him, I suppose. Wasn't it.

Don't start that again. She looked suddenly bored –

bored and also contemptuous – but she had known immediately what he was referring to, it occurred to him.

She turned back to the dishes. He said to the back of her head:

You might as well tell me. She must have had a father, after all.

Suddenly she said:

Where *is* Sally?

She went out of the kitchen and he heard her go into the other rooms. Then she ran up the stairs to the studio. After a moment he heard sounds he could make no sense of and went up after her.

When he reached the top of the stairs he found her holding the child and shaking it vigorously.

She didn't do any harm, he protested.

You must not do that, must not do that, she was shouting. How many times have I told you.

She pushed the child away and as she did so struck it on the side of the head so that it staggered. It looked up at her in surprise, timidly, and then began to scream.

He was frightened by her face. It was white and intense. She hit the little girl on the head again.

For fuck's sake, he cried. What are you doing.

She knows she's not allowed to come up here, she shouted.

He seized her arm but she shook herself free.

You'll hurt her. How fucking often do you do that.

The little girl was frightened and yet she was now

clinging to her mother. And looking at him over her shoulder as if he was the cause of her fear.

Mind your own business. It's nothing to do with you.

She cradled the child in her arms, rocking backwards and forwards. Get out, she said over her shoulder.

I suppose I was confused about something I was experiencing for the first time. I felt pain on her behalf. When she had been hurt it pained me. Yet there were times when I wanted to inflict pain on her. I even thought she wanted me to. But that pain hurt me – although the hurt was like a pain you sometimes inflict on yourself, pleasant as well as painful.

He said:

Why can't Alison look after her?

I can't keep asking her. She has her own life.

Keep asking her? How often does she do it?

Often enough.

When? You're always telling me you can't do anything because of the kid.

Keep your voice down, she said. She's sleeping now.

They were in the kitchen. He closed the door and said:

You're using her as an excuse. For not seeing me.

Make up your mind, she said. One moment you're accusing me of neglecting her and the next, of spending too much time with her.

Don't be stupid.

Often at night – especially when the pulse drummed in his forehead and his face burned – he walked eastward to where the motorway wound like a shiny eel through the centre of the city.

On the way there and back he was calmed by the blackness of the streets where few lamps worked, throwing shining pools on the wet pavements and tarmac of the road. Pacified by the cool rain on his face – for at night it was always raining.

At the great intersection nearby he looked down at the orange-lit gulf, standing on a parapet high above the irregular roar of the traffic, drawing strength from it: the steady glow of the sodium lights, the white lights dutifully following the path marked out for them. And often the sudden and desperate in- and out-breathing of an ambulance or police-car's siren.

Or for a different kind of sustenance, he walked westward towards the parks and terraces and squares where the quietness comforted him.

He said:

Why do you do these things.

She said:

I'm going to die. I don't see that it matters whether it's soon or late.

You stupid bitch, he said. What about the kid.

To see her injured or in pain sent him into a rage. Even the slight grazes that she had not been able to hide from him on this occasion. She said she had been knocked off her bicycle by a careless pedestrian.

She'd probably be better off if I was dead.

You stupid fucking bitch, he said.

CHAPTER THIRTEEN

THE SKY WAS cloudless, pale blue. They followed the path up the side of the ridge and as they breasted it the sheet of water lay glinting, a few hundred yards below them. Up here the landscape stretched flatly into a distant haze that might have been heat. It was too austere for beauty, too remote from his own countryside of farms and villages. She liked it, though it was not hers either. In this part of the country the place-names were as strange to her as to him.

As they began to cross the heather he said:

I didn't get it. They told me on Friday.

She said gently:

You should have.

Perhaps it's just as well.

She asked him what he meant.

Things are difficult enough as it is, he answered. I don't think I could take on any more. In fact, I need to ease back a bit.

They reached the edge of the water whose surface was metallic grey. There was no wind and the water rippled like the veins on the back of an ancient hand. Beyond he could see the glitter of other waters. No trees barred his view or afforded shelter when the wind blew. He shivered. The clarity of the light gave the landscape the vividness of a dream.

She suddenly exclaimed with a smile of pleasure, of delight in her own perverseness, that seemed to him quite child-like:

I'm going in.

You can't. It's frozen.

Of course I can.

It's literally frozen.

He kicked with his toe at some thin ice that had formed along the edge.

But already she had taken off her outer coat and was peeling off her thick jersey. He breathed in heavily, riding with the surge of anger. He felt that her stupidity and wilfulness were intended to annoy him. But at the sight of her expression of eager intensity he understood that her unselfawareness was genuine and her action was not designed to hurt him.

He took her clothes one by one as she handed them to him. Her body was startlingly white and so thin that it hurt. Yet her nakedness made *him* feel vulnerable, as if he was not able to bare *his* body to the cold.

When she was naked she slapped her arms round her body and stood at the side of the loch smiling at him gleefully. Then she stepped into the water. It came up only to her knees and after a few steps she fell forward splashing and gasping. He heard faint cheers and saw three figures waving on the opposite shore. She waved back at them and then swam a few strokes with an expression of rapt intentness. The boys, who were wearing anoraks and woollen hats, cheered again.

So I did get to the mountains in the end, though as it turned out, that was to be the only occasion. And it was hardly what I had anticipated on my arrival. Hardly the trip I had talked about to Lena that first evening there.

The guest-house did not offer dinner. They walked through the streets of the gaunt town that had withdrawn into itself for the winter. The only place open was a big hotel.

They sat alone in the vast, chilly dining-room while the elderly waitress bustled about them.

Don't let's eat too much, she whispered.

Later she asked him:

Have you got any change? I want to ring Kate and John.

He said:

Don't be silly. It's only been a day. What can possibly have happened to her?

She got up from the table and walked towards the lobby.

How could I have known? Was I responsible for what happened? It wasn't my job to foresee the unforeseeable.

She sat naked on the bed watching him undress, one leg raised on which she leaned an arm, one breast pressed against her thigh. The awkward inelegance of the angle of her legs excited him. It was as if she was unaware of the swelling darkness below her flat belly which drew him across the room to crouch over her legs, then nuzzle the soft inside of her thighs and plunge, ignoring her face, into the moist blackness, his tongue seeking the familiar shapes, his fingers squeezing the tips of her breasts.

Tonguing her, himself stiffening, he was aware of her stroking the back of his neck, then he felt her hand moving down his shoulders and sides towards the back of his thigh, then pulling him gently round so that he turned himself, still licking, until his knees were planted in the long hair that spread across the pillow, his hands now caressing her slim thighs.

He heard her sigh quietly and knew she was stroking her breasts with one hand. The other was moving up his belly, the fingers drawing their tips against his skin. In a moment he felt her tongue curving round, her teeth sliding softly up his length, her hands steady on his thighs.

No, he said suddenly. They both froze. After a few moments he felt her lips moving again, the tip of her tongue sliding in and out of her mouth against him.

She said:

I want you in me.

Almost reluctantly, he withdrew and moved round to grip her slender thighs, sliding his hands up so that they cupped her buttocks. He rubbed his chest against her hard breasts in the way she liked, then mumbled their tips between his teeth.

Yes, yes, she whispered, turning her head restlessly.

He raised his hips and came down on her so that, unaided, his cock slid into her.

Hard! she cried.

They intertwined their legs, her calves straining against the back of his to push him further in. He rode down on her while she pulled him into her and they fucked each other.

Once their eyes met, wide and frightened at seeing strangers, it seemed to him, hers mirroring his own. The thought excited him and he held her gaze, slipping from her, his hands on her haunches making his intention clear.

She crouched on the floor, her head against the carpet, her buttocks raised. His stiff bruise brushed against the peach-like swelling, increasing its ache. There was one way to assuage its pain.

He realized that the movements of her body were sobs.

What's wrong?

Her voice came, strange, after a silence:

Why do you want to humiliate me?

What do you mean?

This is how you think of me, isn't it?

He knelt beside her where she lay on the floor and stroked her shoulder.

Don't touch me!

She rolled away from him. He seated himself on the bed. She bored him now.

Where's all this come from?

She turned her face red and distorted by her crying and he saw that she was ugly.

You know very well.

I don't.

You make use of me.

She was ugly and he wanted to hurt her.

I don't know what you mean.

You despise me, don't you? You don't take me seriously. My work.

What are you talking about.

You think my painting's a hobby.

You're being very childish, he said.

I'm just a diversion for you.

Don't be silly, he said. Then:

I'm going to sleep now.

Just something you fuck.

He rolled over to the other side and pulled the blankets up.

I'm turning the light out.

After some minutes she said:

I don't want to go on seeing you.

He lay awake for a long time. Eventually she got in the other side. He slept badly, each time he woke aware of her wakefulness.

In the morning they took the train back, addressing each other only when necessary. She avoided his eyes, her face swollen and red. He spoke to her coldly but, he considered, with more dignity than she.

Once, sitting beside her in front of strangers, he saw how funny it was and started laughing. She didn't look at him.

When they reached the city she went quickly ahead out of the station. He followed her into the Underground. Instead of getting off at the stop nearest to his flat he rode on to hers, a little further for him to walk. As they came out into the street she walked off without looking back.

He wouldn't ring her this time. It was up to her to make the first move. Yet because it seemed to him to have been a misunderstanding he felt he sacrificed nothing. Nevertheless he didn't telephone.

At first it was good to have time to fuck other girls again. There was a very young one called Cindy. She was English. A student. Her lean body was as hard as a boy's. This, with her acrid enthusiasm, enabled and encouraged ways of making love he hadn't tried. And he rang Joanne back at last.

He knew he was flying too high. It excited him that he might get caught out. That he might get burned like Willi. Or even Paul.

He was eating a chop. Lamb or pork. His fork encountered something soft. It was between the fat and the meat. From that layer, at his knife's nudging, it popped out: a fat white maggot. He began to vomit and up from his stomach came an unending stream of monstrous worms and maggots – all brightly coloured and some with billowing, feathery tails.

He had worked late. The darkness would have soothed his headache but it was disconcertingly cut by the flashing strobes. He had seen the girl as he came in. She seemed to be alone.

He moved towards her jerking his body in time with hers. Unsmiling, she answered the movements of his body with her own. Her lean thighs in the tight jeans aroused him.

He leant forward and shouted into her ear:

I'd like to fuck you. Tell me your name.

She turned away. He thought he'd lost her but she turned back. She told him she was called Cindy. Later he asked if she wanted a drink.

She said:

Have you got transport?

The disco was in a warehouse in a back street. He'd left

his car nearby. They drove to her flat in the University district.

She shared it with three other students. When she opened her door he saw two single beds. She said:

If she's not back now she won't be.

When they'd fucked he slept in the other bed.

It was about then that Magnus said to him:

Telling isn't sure that you're carrying your own weight.

He wouldn't say any more than this. He said it to him when they were alone for a moment just before the start of a meeting. He had no chance to press him on it. And later he didn't want to bring it up again in case he had misunderstood.

Sleep had turbulent depths into which he sank each night, surrendering to the restless tides which tugged him fretfully to and fro until he was yanked to wakefulness by the hysterical summons of his alarm.

The food he ate formed itself into a hard pellet inside his gut.

As well as staying late, he was arriving earlier. Often he was at his desk when the cleaners came in. He ate biscuits there for his breakfast. Sometimes he forgot to shave.

He had called on Joanne. She said:

I suppose I can't have any pride. But come in.

When he left work late he often drove to her flat a few streets away and ate what she had prepared for him. She watched him, sometimes eating a little with him, but she had usually eaten earlier. If he wasn't too tired they made love and occasionally he stayed. But he preferred to go home, for the rhythmless noise of the traffic along her main road, which had soothed him once, now kept him awake or, worse, jerked him abruptly up from sleep.

At other times, when he went to Cindy's flat, he found it quiet enough to sleep. If the other girl was there he slept on a mattress between the beds. On those occasions they made love with the light off.

Until once she came in late and finding them, said:

I'll leave the light on if you like.

She watched them while she undressed. And they watched her watching them. She turned away to remove her bra, pulled a nightdress over her head and then removed her pants.

They invited her to join them, but she shook her head.

She went on watching them from her own bed.

CHAPTER FOURTEEN

AT LAST HE telephoned:

I want to see you.

He had time to wonder if the phone would be put down.

There was a pause. Then she said simply:

I want to see *you*.

Her voice moved him as it always did: wistful, vibrant. Only now did he realize how much he had missed her.

It seemed very simple, but he knew it wasn't. He saw her large eyes, veiled slowly by the heavy lids, imagined her waiting, felt an access of tenderness. They agreed on a time to meet.

In the candlelight her face was softened into extreme youthfulness. The hair was spread like a black halo on the pillow. As he looked down at her she ran her hand slowly over his chest and said:

Do you forgive me?

Why do I need to forgive you?

Because I behaved badly.

He didn't answer.

I've behaved badly and I need to be punished.

She cried out, as if angrily:

Punish me.

He came into her hard:

Is this punishment enough?

On the opposite wall their shadows moved, huge and ill-defined, as if independently of them.

No, that's not punishment. That's good.

She tried gently to push him away.

I want you to hurt me.

No, he said.

Hit me.

He reflected that she didn't ask why he had telephoned her.

As she climaxed she cried out:

I love you. I love you. I love you.

Afterwards she said:

Why didn't you hit me when I asked you to?

He kissed her, feeling pity rather than affection.

Let's sleep now, he said. Blow it out.

The candle was on the floor on her side of the mattress. She pursed her mouth and blew out her cheeks with the unselfconscious intentness of a child, took aim and expelled the air.

Out of the darkness he heard:

Have you been having other women?

After a few moments she said:

I don't mind if you have.

Almost asleep, he heard her say, like a child and speaking to herself:

I knew you'd come back. I knew you loved me.

He felt that he had no choice but to perform his quota of actions each day whose meaning it was not for him to concern himself with. That if he followed the rules he would soon be released, even though decisions he had made were beginning to reveal their consequences.

Sleep, not food or drink or sex, had become the physical pleasure towards which he looked forward most eagerly. But sleep was elusive and had to be stalked, often for weary hours. Rarely did it come quickly when he turned off the light and laid his head against the pillow, making himself feel that he was falling softly from one net to the next, each giving way in succession, until he fell right away from himself.

Yet he woke up hardly less exhausted than when he had gone to sleep. At the end of the day the stairs he had to climb seemed impossibly high. Though it now stayed light until tea-time, it was, with cruel humour, getting steadily colder. He felt that the thin membrane inside him whose purpose was to protect him from the outside world, was getting torn so that something raw and tender extruded.

Queuing in a shop, required to endure the slowness, the hesitations, of the people before him, he had to force himself to hold back a scream. In crowded streets, resenting the pedestrians who got in his way, he found he wanted to shoulder them aside. In department stores he sometimes barged into people under cover of the press, his fists bunched, held at his sides. Rats he thought, rats crowded together, biting each other's necks.

Quickly the pattern reasserted itself. He resented her withholding, felt his impulse to tenderness choked off.

Once he realized she'd been crying. Her cheeks wet.

What's the matter.

He took her elbow but she moved it away impatiently.

Nothing to do with you.

He felt he was withdrawing. An instinct for safety had begun remorselessly to operate.

Peter had said to him:

Magnus says Telling wonders if you're main-lining or side-lining.

He said:

I'm giving it everything. They must know that.

I don't need you, she said and turned away.

She had spoken with the insouciance he thought he loved but now he felt he wanted to hurt her. What right had she to exclude him so abruptly?

I don't even know what we're quarrelling about, he said.

That's the trouble, she said.

And more than once she would not make love when he wanted to.

Always tired when they met, they rubbed against each other like two blistered fingers. Made love perfunctorily or not at all. Or fell asleep, waking later, his body straddling hers, his prick still hard inside her.

How could I find the time? Not just the time but the energy, the concentration. At that stage in my career – in what I thought then was to be my career – I had to give it everything I had.

Once he said:

Talk to me. Tell me what's important to you.

She looked at him in surprise. Then her slow arrogant smile twisted her mouth.

She said:

Sally. My work.

He studied her face across which the busy light from the fire cast moving shades and glowings. She bit her lip. After some time she said:

And you.

Then she smiled at him mischievously.

He knew he didn't love her any more. He had watched her closely, seeing her settle back into an assumption of security. She squatted on the floor now with the child slumbering against her knees and thighs, scuffing the heavy skirt up, but unerotically for her knees – vulnerable despite their thick black stockings – and her absorption in the chubby face, the thumb in the mouth, made her seem very frail. In her thin face and high cheek-bones he saw sickeningly the shape of her stripped skull. *When?* he asked himself.

He imagined going away suddenly, never seeing her again. He wanted to hurt her. Perhaps lure her to an appointment – far away – and not turn up. Ring off when she telephoned. Not let her in if she came to the flat.

He wondered why he imagined these things. Why he wanted to see disbelief then pain on her face.

Eventually he bought a trap and placed it on the sideboard where the pellets occurred most thickly.

Setting it was like stretching a nerve taut, creating a small but relentless nemesis. When he put a plate down too hard a foot away it snapped with blind viciousness.

A figure took shape in the mist ahead. Its stance suggested invitation. Now in a close-up he recognized the lumbering body, shoulders half-hunched, the face, though, still shadowed. But the smile. The leer of complicity. Had Paul ever grinned at him like that?

He tried to talk to her. He said:

What went wrong?

But she shook her head vigorously. I don't want to discuss it.

He persisted but she refused.

Talking's no use. What's the good of talking?

He didn't try further, though he felt that if he could understand why she had reacted as she had then he could salvage something.

But he wondered, did he want to?

Something grew in him, something beyond the deep shadows that followed him as he made his way to and fro across the streets between his flat, work, hers, the restaurants, cinemas and bars they visited. Often as he walked alone his legs seemed to be moving to no effect, fixed on one spot while the streets and buildings slid cumbersomely past. Something dark so that when he stopped suddenly, behind his panting he heard another gasp. Moved on quickly, expertly spanning dog-shit and vomit-splashes across the paving-stones, afraid to look back.

It was a big flat in the next street to Lucy's. Kate and John were her oldest friends, she had told him. If that was true, he wondered that he had not met them before. She had been their baby-sitter often enough, she said, so they wouldn't mind the child.

They had had friends for dinner but they had just gone, and, as if roused to an unsatisfied sociability, they seemed now determined to talk. Kate handed him a glass of wine, looking at him curiously.

Did you enjoy it?

He muttered something.

He hardly noticed the story or the actors, so much was his attention over their shoulders, through the windows of the cars, of the apartments. Always against the unchanging blue, the sharply-defined depth impressed him – of the buildings, the tree-lined suburban roads and the extravagant gardens, the wide highways. The evocation of warm nights in the rich darkness disquieted him.

When they came out into the street she gripped his arm.

Shall we take a taxi? he asked.

We'll walk, she said. It's only smirring.

Now the husband came over:

Lucy's been keeping you out of sight.

And you, he answered. I've wondered if I'd ever meet you.

He saw this annoyed her. He added:

She likes to keep her secrets.

She said:

Don't start that again. What about *your* secrets? Then to John she said:

I'll go and get Sally, if that's all right.

She went out.

Is that yours? he asked, indicating one of the canvases.

No, that's far too good. That's one of Don's. Do you know his work?

A little. But all of this is right out of my territory, I'm afraid. Then he said:

You taught Lucy, didn't you?

John nodded.

What do you think of her work?

He looked at the painting for several seconds, almost as if he hadn't heard the question. Then he said:

She's like a lot of young painters in this city.

As if to rescue the ambiguity, he added:

I mean, she hasn't worked through Don's influence. She hasn't worked him out of her system yet.

When they heard Lucy coming down the stairs they moved towards the door. John went ahead.

David, Kate said in an undertone. She stopped and half-turned back to him.

Will you telephone me soon?

He nodded. She was good-looking but ten years too old.

It's the injustice of it. What I did was harmless enough. No worse than many. Nobody ought to have got hurt. It wasn't to be expected that I should foresee everything.

He thought it was finishing – he hoped painlessly. This was confirmed by that dark afternoon they walked along the canal.

It was a dead finger that ran into the centre, here elevated above the surrounding roads – elsewhere a brick-lined gully. Because of the deep locks Lucy held the child's hand, having to run sometimes to keep up with her.

They passed the ancient wharves, wide and still intricately cobbled. The warehouses were demolished –

rubble-strewn wildernesses – or stood, five-storeyed, huge and dark above them, their windows broken, barred on the lower floors.

From up here a large part of the city was visible, dramatically heightened by the dusk and mist shutting off the view beyond. In every direction streets – indicated only by the lines of roofs – marked out the corrugations of the wide valley over which it had been built. As the hills rose and fell like the grey waves of a motionless sea, there was borne in upon him an awareness of its vastness and anonymity. With what intimate part of himself was this city of legendary cruelty connected?

Lucy and the child held hands at the edge of the bank and peered into the water. He saw suddenly a family, safety. But he knew also that this was a temptation, and one to which he would not capitulate. They walked on, their feet crunching on the gravel in the silence through which the sounds of the nearby traffic came muted but clear.

Aren't you afraid, he said. Aren't you afraid.

Afraid of what?

Afraid.

He tried to tell her about the sense of precariousness he felt, about how he kept seeing Paul.

What do you mean, 'seeing' him?

He tried to explain but she seemed perversely not to want to understand him. Something he said appeared to have triggered another train of thought in her.

She let the child walk on a few yards ahead. Then she said:

You've never asked me to marry you.

He thought: was that all. Was it simply that that she wanted. He felt disappointed by the banality of the situation. He said:

Do you want me to?

She didn't answer for a long time. Then she said:

There was a time when I did.

It was getting dark now. Up here there were no lights but in the city the street-lamps, which had been on for some time, were beginning to emerge. There was no indication that, by the calendar at least, spring was approaching.

How could I have predicted it? Was it my job to foresee the unforeseeable? And yet I can't help blaming myself.

Often when he woke suddenly – especially from a bad dream – he found that his jaws were clenched hard together.

Frequently he lay awake late at night hearing the pathos of a dog barking in the distance. The despair. The misery beyond human imagination, in the barking that went on and on, not knowing what or why, not knowing why it should begin or why it should ever stop.

Most had their hair dyed bright colours. Some had shaved their skulls almost bare. It almost surprised him that he could understand what they were saying, so alien did they seem.

She had quickly left him in the kitchen while he was opening the bottle they had brought. Now he carried two glasses in search of her. He found her in a room which had been draped with brightly embroidered materials, turning it into a large tent – no walls or ceiling visible. Lit by candles, joss-sticks burning.

She was in a group. They were all younger than her but she looked no older than them. To him at least. When he went up to her it seemed to him that they stopped talking.

On the way he asked if Leven would be there. She laughed. He only said it to please her.

He gave her the glass. She took it without looking at his face and turned back to the other students. He tried to join in the conversation but was excluded. She drank several glasses quickly. The boys competed for her attention. As he watched her from a few feet away, her voice grew louder, her gestures wilder.

He went closer and said to her softly:

Do you find me boring?

She turned.

Yes, she said, her blue eyes fizzing at him.

She smiled at him, her head slightly tilted.

You're old, she exclaimed. What am I doing with someone as old as you!

Only six years, he said.

It's more, she said. Much more.

She moved away. He drank more wine. He shouldn't have come. These weren't his people. This wasn't enough. She didn't come to find him. He needed something to get him up. Then he remembered what he had with him and took it now.

A little later he was watching from the other side of the room. She didn't look at him.

Suddenly she exclaimed:

I want to dance!

She put her arms on the shoulder of a boy with close-cropped fair hair marked with a pink streak:

Will you dance with me?

The others stood back as she began to sway her body, eyes half-shut, taking a series of little mincing steps in time to the music. Hands circling at her hips, she backed across the room, the boy following her.

Near him she paused. She placed one hand on the boy's chest as if to hold him away. She ran the other slowly down her body pausing at the hip. She looked down at her legs and languorously gyrated her thighs, though her legs were too thin for the effect she was seeking.

She glanced at him over her shoulder. She said:

Are you enjoying yourself.

You're being very silly.

He saw her face darken quickly before she smiled and moved away.

He poured a glass. The way the wine seemed to make the glass swell out like a purple balloon was so beautiful that he drank it and poured another.

Between him and a group by the door was a young girl who looked at him timidly. She was small and had round, plump features. Her hair was frozen in spikes and there were black rings painted round her eyes. When he smiled she lowered her eyes, but smiling faintly.

In the other room more people were dancing. He saw Lucy and the boy, now leaning against each other, moving their feet slowly together. He tried to see if she was watching him, but the room was too crowded with dancers now. A little later he saw her going out with the boy. She glanced back at him expressionlessly.

When they didn't return he suggested another drink. The girl agreed. He took her to the kitchen then looked in the other rooms. Lucy and the boy were not in the flat.

As they reached his door he could hear the telephone. He didn't hurry. This late it could only be her.

She sounded exultant:

I've been ringing for ages. Where were you?

What do you want?

I'm at home. I didn't let Neil come in.

You can do what you like, he said and put down the receiver.

I was taking a lot of shit at that period of my life. That didn't help. It certainly didn't help.

It was about then that McClymont said to me:

Are you here for the ride?

I said:

What do you mean?

Is it just the ride? Is that what turns you on?

He woke suddenly, hearing a rapid clattering. As he switched on the light in the kitchen he saw something being banged vigorously up and down on the sideboard. When he realized what had happened he went quickly to the sink,. turned on the tap and ran some water. Then he picked up the threshing trap and held it under the surface. The movement stopped almost immediately.

He rang the bell and let himself in. Alison met him in the hall.

She's not here. She got a message to go suddenly.

What's the matter?

Her auntie's ill.

He walked into the sitting-room they shared. Alison's bed-room was next door.

She followed him as far as the door.

She'll not be back tonight.

He sat on the sofa.

Will I make you a cup of tea or something?

She looked worried. He said:

Why not sit down?

She seated herself on the edge of the sofa.

Alison, he said.

What? she said after a moment.

Just that, he said. Alison.

He moved slowly towards her. She stayed where she was, staring at him miserably. He placed one hand gently on the back of her neck. Her face was close to his, her eyes watching him. Her blouse was open at the top. He carefully stroked one finger across the back of her neck. Then he reached out his other hand and undid the next button of her blouse. Then the next and the next. He put both arms round her to undo her bra then pulled it down so that her breasts were free. They were firm and bolder than her expression.

He smiled slightly. Behind her glasses her eyes were afraid. Her face was too rounded and boyish to be pretty, but her features were pleasant. He guessed how much she wanted to fuck and her timidity excited him.

He leaned forward. She seemed to think he was going to kiss her and moved her head back slightly, perhaps worried about her glasses. But his head went lower and his teeth closed tenderly on one smooth nipple.

His face felt flushed. He wondered if it was the heating. The air was cool against it but when he got inside the building it was still hot.

And the slight but constant ache around his temples.

I've not been back since then. There's nothing there for me now. You can't dwell in the past. It's history now.

The rain had stopped before they left his friends' flat and the sky was clear. There was nobody about. The street curved slightly as it climbed a steep ridge overlooking the river, and when they reached its top a large part of the city lay before them. The stars seemed to be hanging a few hundred feet above him. Among them he noticed a red light. It flashed on and off.

It took an effort to attend to her. She was saying:

There's only one thing about it that annoys me.

On one side there was a gap where a tenement building had been demolished. He let her walk on without him and watched the red light – and now he could see the green – unhurriedly winking, moving only in relation to the stars.

He heard her stop and come back a few steps.

And that's that you've lost me a good lodger.

Now its sound came rolling steadily towards him in waves, and he could see it – at first only as it blotted out stars but then as an illuminated shape itself. It seemed hardly to be moving, its sound echoed from somewhere else, and he watched it mesmerized until its lighted fuselage passed above him as smoothly as a submarine above the floor of an ocean.

She said impatiently:

I warn you, if you behave like that then so will I.

Then she said:

Hurry up.

He said to Magnus:

I'm being side-lined.

Magnus didn't answer. He said again:

They're side-lining me. Aren't they.

He knew he was bored with her. The things that had delighted him he now saw as irritating mannerisms or, worse, affectations. He thought about her still when they were apart, but his anticipation was always disappointed by the reality. When he kissed her he was trying to find what he had felt before. She misunderstood and kissed him passionately back.

Yet their love-making was better than ever. He would fuck her, unable to climax or to stop, until they were both exhausted.

The jaw absurdly flapping so that the lipless teeth kept jamming together, the blank sockets keeping their secrets, it came spidering across the carpet. In the half-light stood people laughing. Paul, his rounded shoulders jerking. It almost touched his feet.

He was wet, his heart thumping. He turned on the lamp.

Perhaps it didn't end. But that was what was waiting.

He lit a cigarette. The silence was complex, multilayered.

CHAPTER FIFTEEN

THE OCCASIONAL SIGHT of the sun and the mild warmth seemed like an aberration. It was an invasion to which the city only gradually yielded. In these brief intervals there appeared bare knees and thighs, arms and shoulders, ice-cream pale as if freshly unbandaged.

He hardly noticed for he pruned away everything that wasn't relevant to getting him to work and keeping him at it. Now that the system wasn't working out well, he felt that Magnus and the others were avoiding him. But because *he* was avoiding *them* he rarely went to the bar now so he wasn't sure. When he did go it was always late and he drank quickly in order to get to sleep as soon as he got home.

He came in for most of the week-end, working alone in the silent building – probably the only person in it for much of the time. He was in a sustained panic – attempting at this late stage to rescue things as if trying to assemble a jig-saw – but there was no jig-saw for there was no picture.

He didn't ring her. He didn't think about it. There was nothing more to it than that. He didn't ring her, and she didn't get in touch with him.

He felt tired yet restless. Repressed energy and violence were building up inside him. He felt he needed to run, to hit the pavements hard and malevolently, to run himself into a state of exhaustion. But always it was raining as he walked home.

He didn't telephone first but went straight round. When Joanne opened the door he could see she was hostile. But even before he spoke she saw something in his face and told him to come in.

He got what he wanted. He lay on her thick rug with his shoes and jacket off while she stroked him. He was too tired to eat or to talk. She murmured into his ear a summary of what had happened to her since the last time. They drank brandy. It wasn't sex he wanted, it was this.

The cat lay purring against one of his feet. He could feel its vibration through his sock.

He washed his hands. The surface of the water was reflected on the side of the bowl, a golden dappling against the white enamel. His hands were reluctant to relinquish the warm water. He held his gaze down to avoid the mirror. Somewhere behind his eyes the pain clenched and unclenched. This place had its own rhythm: the steady blast of the extractor, the regular whifflings of the flush.

He ran the cold tap and splashed the cool water over his hands, each serving the other. Behind him the double doors swung suddenly and someone came in. He looked cautiously into the mirror. It was McClymont. He advanced unbuttoning himself, moving each leg awkwardly in turn to keep the zip straight.

He pulled out the plug and moved towards the dryer, shaking his hands. The warm blast brought its own excited note of summons to the world outside. He rubbed his hands slowly together watching McClymont's elbow jerking as he delicately finished. McClymont ran both taps full on and splashed his hands perfunctorily, then cupped them and, bending forward, squashed his face into the palms, shaking his head and blowing out through his mouth and nose as the water ran down his beard. He came over to the dryer holding out his hands, the sleeves of his shirt and jacket drawn back.

He wondered if he was watching him. If he had been told to follow him in here.

His hands refused to dry. The machine stopped suddenly and he restarted it. He and McClymont stared at each other while the dryer roared and the plumbing hissed and gurgled.

He would have passed her without noticing if they had not met under a lamp. He caught her face turning towards him. She was between two men who were half-supporting her, half-propping themselves against her. She was laughing but as she turned to him the laughter faded, the eyes going dead and the cheeks hollowing sullenly.

For God's sake!

She stopped and the two men walked on as if unaware.

What?

Her face was bruised on one side and there was dried blood on it.

What's happened?

You haven't rung me.

She was making an effort to hold steady but swayed as she spoke.

Who are those men?

They had stopped some distance ahead and were looking back.

It's none of your business.

What the hell's going on?

She turned and saw that the two men had started again.

I've got to go. My friends are waiting.

Where to?

She began to walk away. He seized her arm:

Where are you going, for Christ's sake?

She turned quickly and shook the arm free.

Don't you touch me. What right have you got to touch me?

He advanced a step and she backed away holding up her arm to shield her face. The fear was unfeigned. She was bowed forward slightly, her legs bent at the knees, her blood-smeared face held up to him. Then she turned and ran along the pavement, her hips in the tight skirt jerking from side to side in an ungainly lollop. As she reached the two men she glanced back quickly. Then she pushed between them and put her arms up to their shoulders. He watched them until they turned the corner.

And yet if she had been honest with me. I hid nothing from her. By which I mean that she never asked me anything about which I needed to lie. But I have to admit that she didn't lie to me. She just kept the truth from me.

As she stared at him her face seemed large, the jaw heavy and almost brutal.

She said:

What do you think gives you the right?

They were sitting in her kitchen. She didn't offer him anything. He was too tired to argue. He didn't want a scene. He had just come from work. He wanted to cause her pain, to get revenge for what she had put him through. He wondered how he had ever thought she was beautiful: her cheekbones too high, her mouth thin and selfish. The deep cut and the bruise around it angered him.

I don't *need* you, she said. She seemed to be speaking to herself.

He said, making an effort to stop his voice quavering, but whether with regret or triumph he wasn't sure:

Let's be quite calm about this. Let's just say we'll stop seeing each other.

He could see that she was taken by surprise by this.

Her face seemed to narrow as she scrutinized him. Now suddenly the amazing eyes with their heavy brooding lids and thick lashes, her thin wrists twisting nervously on the table, the injury to her face, cut deep into his belly.

She said:

Is that what you want?

Don't *you*?

All right then, go.

She stood up. He followed her through the hall where she opened the front-door.

Goodbye, then.

She didn't answer. Her features were impassive as she closed the door after him.

Often, late at night, he would walk into an area of the city nearby that was waiting to be cleared. Here the street-lamps no longer functioned. The empty and half-ruined tenements seemed larger in the moonlight. Along the rows of dark and often shattered windows there would sometimes be one light still showing. An old man or woman, perhaps, refusing to be budged.

Or, as the evenings lengthened, he would climb a steep hill overlooking the park around which terraces spiralled, and from the balcony that encircled its summit, he would look out over the whole city: the river, the docks, and the airport far away.

From up here the stars seemed to be drawn past as if cranked on a roll.

I don't know how long it was after that that the next thing happened. I lose track of time because of the pressure I was under at that period. To be frank, I didn't think about her much because I didn't have the time.

That was when it all went wrong. I think I realized it before most of the others. It was all falling to pieces in my hands. The more I tried to pull it together the more I pulled it apart. And then my own panic turned into a general panic that terrible day.

What do I remember of it? People shouting down phones. People not getting through. The technology failing and becoming suddenly so many wires and plugs and monitors. The screens going blank – not blanked out which would have been bad enough, but still illuminated and staring, brightly vacant, relentlessly, menacingly.

I remember Magnus shouting, unshaven and his tie out of place, ordering one of the secretaries to stay as long as he required her. Even Telling jacketless and short-tempered. We worked through the night trying to salvage something. When Tokyo came on-line we knew immediately that it was all over. Then at just before ten that morning we heard about Telling.

Nothing was his own now. Suddenly he seemed to be no more than a visitor. The flat, his car. Even his desk. Particularly his desk.

In shops, at the office, he was almost surprised to be greeted by anyone. In this city, he no longer felt he existed.

I suppose the truth is you can keep a thing under for so long, but then it bobs up again. Somebody once said that and I think it's true. In fact, I suppose that's what I've learned.

Still, I suppose it's ancient history now.

He couldn't blame Magnus, he supposed, but he felt badly treated by the others. By Telling in particular, and also Hewison, Lloyd, McClymont. In fact, he supposed now that Magnus had tried to warn him.

A lot of money was involved. Of course, it wasn't only down to him. Nobody could have predicted how the system would behave under those conditions. But then, he supposed, you could say he was paid to predict that.

This was the end of the line. In a way he was relieved. The pressure would soon be off. He felt he'd learned a lot. In future he would do things differently.

The summer couldn't be far away now.

By the time he was even half-awake he had the receiver in his hand.

This is Kate. Kate Gurney.

He muttered something. The name meant nothing to him.

Lucy's friend from Cecil Street.

I was asleep.

I got your name from the book. You never rang me. I wanted to talk about Lucy.

What about her?

She was having trouble coping with the child. After Alison left, it got worse.

He muttered something and she said:

Look, I'm very worried about her.

What's the matter?

She was round here earlier to collect Sally. She was behaving very strangely. She left about midnight and I've been ringing her since then but she's not answering.

I haven't seen her for nearly a month.

There was a pause.

She said she'd seen you today.

She said what?

That she'd seen you today.

He didn't answer and she said:

I think you'd better go round.

As he let himself in he could hear raised voices. He groped his way across the hall in near-darkness. There was no light except for a narrow shaft at the half-opened door of the small bedroom in which the child slept. He listened for a moment and realized that it was only one voice he had heard – shouting incomprehensibly then dropping to a low murmur. He didn't recognize it. At regular intervals there was a sharp crack.

He went into the room. There was not much light because the lamp had fallen on to its side, and was partly covered by the bed which had been pushed away from the wall. Where the bed had been the child was propped against the wall. Her mother, her back to the door, seemed to be holding her up and doing something that he couldn't see. His first thought was that they were playing a game. For a moment he wondered what the dark pattern on the child's night-shirt was. Then as she swung her arms again he saw how the noise he had heard was being made.

He gripped her by the shoulders and pulled her back. As her face swung round, he saw the blue eyes immense and empty, the pupils tiny points.

The child had fallen to the ground and lay like a broken doll.

CHAPTER SIXTEEN

WHEN EVERYTHING WAS ready he checked that he still had the empty packet. He had left himself just time to get another.

The stairs were dim and cool and when he got out on the pavement he was unprepared for the heat which had built up since earlier in the morning. Few people were on the streets. The shops looked as if they were shut up, for the sun's glare made their interiors dark.

As he turned the corner into the great wide street that ran into the centre, a slight breeze for a moment filled out his shirt. For as far as he could see in either direction until sight was lost in the haze, nothing moved except a solitary bus. It was the beginning of the summer fair.

A small boy and girl sat on the steps outside Murphy's. He passed its doors without nostalgia.

The shop was empty. In the gloom at the back he needed the dim lights to find what he wanted. He paid Mrs Iqbal, fanning herself on her chair behind the till. Carefully carrying the two boxes, he was half afraid that his moist hands sticking to their cellophane wrappings would tear them.

Now he had made himself late. He scribbled a note and left it under one of the boxes on the kitchen-table. Relieved that he had so little time, he went quickly into each room for a final check.

The windscreen had acquired a coating of fine dust. He searched for the washer-button and for a moment the street and the sky became a blurred pattern of blue and grey, until he activated the wipers.

Kate's directions, written on the empty cigarette-packet, took him straight there. Through the gate to one side was a tall Victorian building, almost every window shattered. Ahead was an arrangement of single-storeyed boxes.

He left the car and followed the appropriate signs, which led him into a wide low corridor with a brightly-polished floor – a dimly-lit windowless tunnel. He passed through a succession of swing-doors. When he found the right place he reported to the office.

Are you sure it's all right? he asked.

The severity of the face was enhanced by the uniform:

Yes. She should see people.

How much does she remember?

Very little. Don't stay long.

I can't anyway. I have a flight in less than an hour.

You'll find her in the day-room straight ahead.

As he turned away the nurse said:

And don't talk about what happened.

He passed through another swing-door into a narrow lobby. Opposite was a glass wall with a door to one side. Through the glass he saw a bare room with a few chairs and tables scattered about. A television stood against the further wall, its colours badly-tuned: a cartoon cat, greenish-red, chased a faintly-purple mouse.

There was only one person in the room, sitting in the middle watching the screen, but it couldn't be her because the hair was too short. Then the figure half-turned as a nurse came in through a door at one side, and he realized that her hair had been cropped. The nurse did something to the television and then went over to her. She looked up. They appeared to be speaking.

He went in. As he approached she looked at him but he couldn't interpret her expression. The nurse moved away and went out. The television was still on but no sound came from it.

Hello, he said, wondering if he should kiss the pale forehead now revealed.

Hello, she replied still looking at him as if with nothing more than mild curiosity.

In the long white gown she looked thinner than ever. Her arms were bare below the elbows and the veins blue against the startling white. He pulled a chair nearer and sat down. She ended her scrutiny of him and turned away.

I've brought you these.

She took the chocolates and held them on her lap without looking at them.

Is everything okay here?

She nodded her head once emphatically. Her hands were restlessly clasping and unclasping the box. She was looking past him. He turned and found that her attention was on the silent television.

The box fell from her lap, without her seeming to notice. He picked it up and placed it on another chair.

Shall I turn the sound up?

She didn't answer. He watched her, his eyes drawn to the delicate ear and neck now revealed by the clumsy cutting of her hair.

Suddenly she turned her gaze on to him – those startling depths – and said:

I miss Sally. When will they let me see her?

He said:

I don't know anything about that. You'll have to ask someone else.

The glitter in her eyes seemed to fade and she turned back.

A nurse came in. She smiled at him clinically and said:

You're to come with me now, Lucy.

She didn't turn her head from the screen.

I don't want to, she said petulantly.

Come along.

Her brow furrowed and she seemed about to start crying:

Why must I?

With a hand on her shoulder the nurse gently encouraged her to stand. She turned away without looking at him. Leaving the box of chocolates where it was, and with the nurse holding her by the elbow, she walked slowly towards the farther door. He wondered if she would turn back. Just as they reached the door the nurse looked round quickly and nodded to him.

When they had disappeared he went back into the lobby and then walked along the corridor through the first swing-door and then the next and then the next towards the last door and beyond it to where the hired car was parked in the sunlight.